RESERVE MY CURVES:
YOUR HUSBAND CHOSE ME

B.M. Hardin

Dedication

This book is dedicated to all of the sassy, beautiful and curvaceous women out there. Love the skin that you are in! It's an absolute privilege to be a big girl.

Special thanks to Sparkle Nicole for gracing the cover with her curves! Thank you!

Photographer: Carrie Smith of CCMG (Conceited Curves Model Management) Amazing photos and thank you as well!

Acknowledgements

First and foremost, I want to thank my Heavenly Father for my talents and my gifts and each and every story that he has placed in me.

It is an honor and a privilege to be living my dream and walking in my purpose and for that I am forever thankful.

Also to all my family, friends, critiques, supporters, readers and everyone else, thank you for believing in me and allowing me to share my gifts with you.

Your support truly means the world to me!

B.M. Hardin

Author B.M. Hardin's contact info:

TEXT BMBOOKS to 22828 for more release updates

Facebook: http://www.facbook.com/authorbm

Twitter: @BMHardin1

Instagram: @bm_hardin

Email:bmhardinbooks@gmail.com

RESERVE MY CURVES

Chapter ONE

"You want me to do what?"

"Envy calm down. It's not as bad as it sounds. You act like it's the end of the world or something. One of our *guests*, one of the richest men in the world, specifically asked for. Well...he requested you. He caught sight of you on his way in. Trust me, I've been doing business with him for a very long time, and he is a hard man to please. He's very picky and very selective. If anything, you should be honored that he even noticed you. And then again, we both know what it is about you that he noticed. You do have those country, biscuit eating hips. A blind man could *see* those curves. Anyway, I informed him that you were one of our *regular* maids, but he insists. I'm sure that you could use the extra money, and I'm talking about a lot of extra money. I'm talking thousands of dollars, just to start."

I sat back slowly in one of her overpriced chairs.

I couldn't believe my ears.

If I didn't know any better I would have thought that she'd just asked me to sleep with one of the hotel guests for money.

No, that just couldn't be what she was saying.

I had to be hearing her all wrong.

"You can consider all of this as something like a *promotion*. Of course, I know how hard things have been for you lately, not to mention that you are a single mother; so, I'm sure that this could help you out. And I've heard that once you go up to the thirteenth floor, you'll never want to come back down here again."

"Thirteenth floor? I thought there were only twelve floors in this hotel."

"Like I said, there are a lot of things that *regular* maids, *regular* employees and *regular* guests don't know about this hotel. But I'm offering you to become a part of our exclusive, executive, group of maids that take care of our top executive guests."

"What would I have to do?"

"Oh, aren't you cute? Sweetie, use your imagination. But the short answer is---you'll do whatever he wants you to do; whatever he *orders*. You'll do a little bit of this and a little bit of that. Ride a little something. Suck a little something else. Basically, it's like room service; with a twist. Trust me Envy, after a while; making this money will be a piece of cake."

Okay, so she has officially lost her damn mind!

I wasn't just a piece of ass on a platter or a steak with a side of *pussy*!

Apparently, she was confused as to the type of woman that I was.

"I'm sorry, but I'll have to decline."

"Envy, think about this. I'm talking about a lot of money here and all you must do is *entertain* a guest for a few hours or so. Everyone is nervous in the beginning but trust me, when you start making more money than you could ever imagine, you'll get over it. They always get over it. But I have a few things to help you along the way. Envy, I can help you get out of your financial troubles, but you must be willing to help yourself. Think about what I'm saying to you."

I sat for a second to take it all in.

I could surely use some extra cash.

But if she wanted to help me out, she could give me a few extra hours or something, instead of trying to convince me to sell my ass.

"I thought about it and I would rather be a *regular* maid. Thanks for the offer, but no thanks," I said standing to my feet.

"I guess we have some kind of misunderstanding. Maybe I didn't exactly make myself clear. You see, either you *will* take the *promotion*…or we no longer need your services," Carmen said with a smirk on her face.

Was she serious?

"What? Are you serious? You're firing me?"

"I'm not doing anything. You're the one making all of the decisions here."

You have got to be kidding me!

She was really going to fire me because I wouldn't sleep around with some rich man for money?

I was the best damn maid this hotel had and she was going to fire me?

Heaven knows, I wanted to smack the hell out of her and knock that shrewd grin off her face but I slammed my work badge down on her desk instead.

She could have this damn job.

I slammed her office door shut behind me and headed to the employees lounge to gather my things.

She'd known better than to even approach me with the proposition in the first place.

She had to have known that I would've declined.

Carmen knew how I felt about men, dating, and even sex, so how dare she approach me with something like that?

She had better be glad that I wasn't a thing like I used to be or otherwise I wouldn't have even hesitated to whoop her ass.

But for now, I would simply walk away with my dignity.

As soon as the glass doors of the hotel closed behind me, reality *pissed* in my face, as I started to walk down the busy streets of Charlotte, NC.

Panic and worry made their presence known, and immediately I started to evaluate my situation.

Did I really just get fired from my job?

I was already up to my neck in bills. I couldn't afford to be unemployed.

What in the hell was I going to do for money?

Envy, what were you thinking?

I knew that declining Carmen's offer was the right thing for me to do, but it didn't feel that way.

Maybe I should have at least considered it.

No, considering becoming a whore just sounded stupid.

Maybe I should have at least tried to reason with her and explain to her how much I needed my job.

But then again, she already knew that.

She already knew that I was struggling.

She already knew how much I needed money.

But she hadn't cared.

Turning around and begging Carmen for my job back would only be a waste of time since I was sure that she wouldn't give a rat's ass about my pleas.

But now what?

What was I going to do?

I only lived about a block and a half away from the hotel so I was home in a flash.

I checked the mailbox and as always, I pulled out a hand full of bills.

I wondered how many of them I would piss off if I sent them checks that I already knew were going to bounce.

But then again, a bounced check would lead to additional fees, and hell, I already didn't have enough money to cover them as it was.

Bills were of the Devil!

Frustrated to the max, I tucked the bills under my arm and prepared to enter the house.

"Damn Envy, only you can make a maid outfit look so damn sexy," my married neighbor, Rodney, bellowed in my direction.

I absolutely hated a married man who cheated on his wife or even flirted with another woman.

I mean it literally made my ass itch!

If you don't want to be married…don't get married!

Damn, it's just that simple!

Yet, some men could care less about the wife that he had at home.

Instead, he was out looking for his next nut.

For the life of me, I just couldn't understand.

And Rodney, my neighbor, was the worst husband on the planet but his wife walked around as though she'd hit the jackpot or something by marrying him.

I couldn't count the number of times that he'd come out his mouth with something perverted or disrespectful towards me, right in front of her, and she would pretend as though she hadn't heard it and say nothing.

But I would say enough for the both of us.

I cursed him out, faithfully, but he acted as though it was all a game.

But it would be a cold day in hell before his old married ass would ever lay a hand on me.

With the last thought running across my mind, I frowned in his direction, stuck up my middle finger, and then turned the knob of my front door.

Cheating bastard!

"Mommy!" Horizon, my daughter, screamed as I entered the living room.

This was always the best part of my day.

Coming home and seeing my beautiful, smiling three-year-old meant the world to me.

I loved her more than words could ever express and I wanted nothing more than to give her the world.

But the truth was that I could barely give her a roof over her head most of the time.

I never imagined having to carry the load of raising her all on my own.

Her father, and my first love, Keymar, died when Horizon was only two months old.

The doctors were unsure as to the exact cause but one morning I rolled over to a cold, dead body.

Overnight, just like that, he was gone.

He'd gone to sleep for the very last time and unfortunately, neither of us had been able to say goodbye.

He was a man in his prime, healthy and in good shape and since the doctors couldn't really explain it, the only logical reason for me was to believe that for whatever reason, it was just his time to go.

So, suddenly, I was forced to raise my child all on my own and it just hasn't been easy.

Keymar and I had been together since our high school years, and because he was raised by old, country folks, he believed that the man was the one who worked, not the woman.

He was the provider, the bread winner and always had been.

He wouldn't have it any other way.

My only job was to stay home, clean, cook and wash his drawers.

And of course, give him the *goods* whenever he asked for them.

But abruptly, all of that had come to an end.

And with a baby to take care of, I had to do what I had to do.

I had to get out and find a job.

For a woman who had never worked a day in her life, finding a job hadn't been easy for me.

Sure, I had a high school diploma but that was it.

I hadn't bothered to go to college.

I hadn't bothered to gain any type of special skills.

I hadn't bothered to do anything except make sure that I took care of home.

And to think that all those years of lounging around the house when I would have nothing to do, I could have at least gotten a higher education or something, whether on campus or online, but I hadn't.

And to this day, I was paying for it.

But someone, somewhere, must have been praying for me because before becoming a maid, I had a few employers actually take a chance on me and hired me although I didn't have one bit of experience.

But guess what; no sooner than I would get comfortable, I would get fired.

Mostly because finding a stable babysitter for my daughter was like open heart surgery…one hell of a task.

I couldn't exactly afford to put her in a *real* daycare, so I found myself depending on undependable, money hungry, family members and family friends.

And because of it, I would end up terminated and on the hunt for employment once again.

Currently, my youngest sister was home from college for the summer, so she'd agreed to babysit for me, for free of course, for the entire summer.

That was one less thing that I was going to have to worry about, but hell, now I was unemployed so it didn't really matter.

The job at the hotel had sort of fell into my lap.

I was literally walking down the street one day, and Carmen stopped me and asked me if I knew anyone looking for work.

I couldn't speak up fast enough.

She'd put me on the schedule the very next day and I'd been at the hotel ever since.

Though it hadn't been the best job, it was something.

And now I'd been fired from there too.

"You're home early," my sister Tia pointed out.

I was the oldest of four girls.

Two of the girls were married and lived in different cities, and Tia, the youngest, was on her way to her last year of college.

I was so proud of her.

Mama passed away her senior year of high school, but she stuck it out and hung in there like a champion.

Now, she was only a school year away from having a degree in Business and I was her biggest fan.

Though she was on a scholarship, and tried to pick up a few work hours as a hostess when she could, time to time I had to make sure that she was okay.

She still needed things and she didn't have anyone else to depend on, except for me, so I had to make sure that I could do little things for her here and there.

I was her big sister and it was my job to look after her.

But trying to take care of her, my daughter and myself on a maid's salary wasn't easy.

I ignored her comment and focused on my daughter for a while longer.

I smiled at her.

She was everything to me.

She was my rainbow after a thunderstorm; my sunshine on a cloudy day.

Had it not been for her, I would have given up a long time ago.

After small talk, a few forced laughs and hesitant giggles, I headed to the kitchen to prepare dinner.

At least food was one thing that I never had to worry about.

Food stamps were the best thing since cooked crack if you asked me!

Seriously, they were one heck of a blessing.

I couldn't speak for those that misused the system, or for those that received them but didn't actually need them. I could only speak for myself and this sista' right here needed every last one of them.

If we didn't have anything else we had food and I found comfort in knowing that my baby was going to get a good, hot meal every single night.

I couldn't even imagine how the struggle would be if food was another expense that was on my shoulders.

Things were already tight enough.

"You got fired, didn't you?"

"Why are you so nosey?"

"Why are you so secretive?"

I got that a lot.

Everyone always said that I was a very private person and that I was very good at keeping a secret but they had no idea how right they were.

"I'll be just fine," I said to my sister with a smile but the truth to the matter was that I felt like crying.

I had about two weeks before everything would be *officially* due and I had no clue as to where to begin looking for work.

I'd been at the hotel for about two years, and though I hated cleaning up after grown ass people, it was a job and it was better than having no job at all.

Things were always tight, and things sometimes went unpaid or on a pay arrangement, but it was more than having nothing.

I couldn't pay bill collectors with *nothing*.

I guess I could go apply for extra assistance.

But they were so stingy with benefits these days that I wasn't sure if I would qualify for much of anything but it was worth a try.

I received a small check for my daughter from Social Security every month, on behalf of Keymar and as a result of his passing, but that would only cover a minor bill or two.

I was going to need a hell of a lot more.

We lived in the house that my parents left behind.

Daddy died a few years before Mama, and it wasn't until he died that Mama learned that the house that she'd thought had been paid off years ago…wasn't.

Daddy had a secret gambling problem that none of us were aware of and he'd taken out a loan on the house to pay off his debt.

He'd kept it hidden from Mama for years and had just been paying the bank back as if nothing was wrong.

Mama retired as a teacher and Daddy had retired from the military, so they both received a decent amount of money each month.

That woman trusted him with every ounce of blood in her body so she never even questioned him about the few hundreds of dollars that he was taking and paying off the bank with on a monthly basis.

She'd said that she assumed that he was simply putting something back for a rainy day or extra to leave behind when he'd reached the end of his road.

But Daddy hadn't left behind a thing but bills and a small life insurance policy.

So, once he passed, Mama paid half of what he owed the bank with the life insurance check that she received, and she took over making the rest of the payments.

And now that she was gone, I didn't have a choice but to try my best to save their home.

It was all that we had left of them.

Yes, Mama had a small life insurance policy as well but we'd used it to remodel the house.

The house was old and needed a ton of upgrades in order for it to be suitable to live in and raise a family.

The payments weren't all that high, so Keymar and I thought that using the extra money to remodel the house was a good idea.

Keymar had a great job driving for a local company and made more than enough money to take care of the house payments and every other expense that we had.

Who knew that he was going to pass away so soon?

The bad part was that we had been in the middle of switching life insurance policies and since the process had never been officially completed, I wasn't able to collect on either policy when Keymar died.

So now, the house payments and everything else were my responsibilities.

The house payments weren't all that much but they were enough; especially when you barely had enough coming in.

But I was trying my best, even when my best just didn't seem good enough.

With the house, money and my parents on my mind, I recalled the last words that Mama had said to me.

"Envy, I had you when I was just a young girl. I had no idea how to be a mother. I was just following around a man in a uniform like I was some little puppy dog. Trying my best to get out of the projects and be better than my folks thought that I would be. Had I had any sense, I surely wouldn't have named you Envy. That's one of the seven deadly sins you know. I don't know what I was thinking. All I knew was that I had a beautiful, precious baby girl that I thought the world of. You grew up to be such a beautiful woman and I'm so proud of you baby. You are going to have an amazing life and an amazing earthly experience. But believe me, Mama will be waiting on you on the other side," Mama had said.

Minutes later, she took her last breath and closed her eyes.

She'd said a mouthful, and had left a hell of a lot to live up to, but I was a fighter.

And just like she'd fought breast cancer for almost ten years, I was here to win.

And I just couldn't give up now.

That night, after I cut my maid uniform into a thousand tiny pieces, I looked out at the stars as I laid restless in my worn out queen-sized bed.

I couldn't help but feel disappointed and maybe even defeated. It seemed as though I was always finding myself between a rock and a hard place.

But something just had to give.

After hours of staring at the sky and finally feeling sleepy, I headed to the window to close the blinds but…

"Ahh!" I screamed at the pair of eyes staring at me.

With my hand on my chest, instead of running away, I took a closer look.

It was my neighbor Rodney.

He'd scared the hell out of me!

And the scariest part of all was that even though he knew that I saw him, he didn't run.

Instead he grinned and then walked away, slowly, as though stalking or peeping through my window wasn't a crime.

I was sick of his ass!

That was the last straw!

The perverted comments, I could handle.

The disrespectful looks, I could deal with.

But peeping through my window was just too damn far!

I tried to stay out of his marriage and not rat his inappropriate ass out to his wife constantly but enough was enough.

Even though I knew that she heard him, maybe it would actually sink in if she heard it from me.

I checked the time to see that it was a little before midnight but I didn't care.

I was going over there.

Getting myself together, I headed down the hallway.

Tia was standing there, watching me, awaiting an explanation for my yells.

I briefly told her and explained to her that if I wasn't back in ten minutes to call the police.

Tia was a little *thuggish* at heart; so, I knew that if they tried anything, the police would be the least of their problems.

Heading next door, I wasn't at all nervous.

If anything, I was pissed off and after the kind of day I'd had, Rodney had picked the wrong time to get on my bad side.

I banged on the front door and instead of Rodney coming to the door, his wife answered it instead.

His wife hardly ever spoke to me and I only assumed that it was because she knew her husband had a thing for me.

But that was her problem.

"Where's Rodney? You tell your husband that the next time I catch his peeping ass in my window, his ass is going to jail!"

His wife didn't say a word.

She simply looked at me as though she didn't believe me.

Rodney appeared and I wanted to push his wife out of the way so that I could smack him in his face.

"If you ever look in my window again, your ass is going to jail. Do you understand me?" I said as harsh as I could.

His wife turned to face him.

"What? You already know I want her. Hell, you want her too," Rodney said to her.

What?

What the hell kind of sick shit is going on over here?

I waited for her to say something to him but she didn't.

"Unless you're going to bring your sexy ass in here and go to bed with us, I suggest you go on back home," Rodney finally said.

I was completely and utterly disgusted!

People today were just plain ole' crazy and it was just my luck that I had a pair of lunatics as neighbors.

But I could get crazy too and I had to make sure that both of them knew that I meant business.

"Don't be surprise if you get a not so friendly visit from the police tomorrow. I just need to make sure that something is on file; just in case you pull something like that again and you end up losing an eye. If you think I'm playing…try me. Stay the hell away from me, my house and my bedroom window. Now you freaks enjoy your night," I said and hurriedly walked away.

Wow, this has been one hell of a day!

The next morning, I woke up with a major headache.

I assumed that it was from having such an awful day the day before with the hotel and the nasty neighbors' next door but I was going to have to shake it off and get started with my day.

I had things to do.

I headed to the room where my sister was sleeping and picked up her laptop.

After secretly connecting to the neighbors Wi-Fi, I headed to the site to file my unemployment.

I wasn't sure as to whether I was supposed to put that I had been fired or that I'd quit.

Both selections were pretty much valid considering the whole ordeal, but I went with the one that was more than likely going to rule in my favor.

I was fired...but I put laid off.

Doesn't really matter that it wasn't exactly the correct term but for Carmen's sake, she had better cooperate or she was surely going to wish that she had.

I needed every little bit of money that I could get in order to keep a roof over my baby's head until I could do better and I would sing like a canary if she tried to deny me of what was rightfully mine.

She didn't want these problems and that was the truth.

I was as sweet as apple pie, but if I was pushed to the edge, I didn't mind reaching out and touching somebody, if you get my drift.

Mama used to say that it was a big sibling thing.

I wasn't sure and I didn't care what they called it. All I knew was that if any of them had a problem, I went running and talking was the last thing that I was coming to do.

Closing the computer, I got myself together and headed out to get a few other things done.

I lived in the city, and where I couldn't walk, I rode the bus.

I had a car, but it needed a new transmission.

It had been broken for quite some time so I wouldn't be surprised if it needed something else by now.

So, it was either my two feet or public transportation.

In all honesty, unless the weather was bad, I didn't mind walking; it kept everything tight and just right.

My daughter had taken me from an eight to an eighteen, well maybe a twenty, and I carried every bit of the extra weight in my hips.

My body was full of curves, speed bumps, and everything else but I loved me some me!

I was well proportioned in all the right places.

From the front, you would have thought that I had an ass the size of Texas... but I didn't.

I had just enough junk in my trunk.

But it was more than enough.

The top half of my body was rather small.

Small breasts, small arms and I didn't have a gut or even a baby-pouch.

I was thick with it; definitely a big girl, but I was in shape though. And baby there was nothing like curves that stayed in place or a plus-sized woman who could walk a runway with confidence beside a woman that was a size two and still look just as good because everything was firm and didn't jiggle.

Yes, I was that woman and I absolutely loved the skin that I was in.

Curves and all, I looked good naked...and really, that was all that really mattered.

I headed up the street wearing sunglasses.

It was barely 9:00 a.m. but the sun was on its A-game. It sat high and shined bright, causing me to immediately forget about looking cute and I proceeded to pull my head full of curls into a ponytail.

But I walked on.

Nothing was going to stop me from trying to get things done.

Finally, I reached the bus stop.

The bus was running late, as usual, but I tried not to become frustrated.

I had more important things to worry about.

I especially had to make sure that I went by the police station. The whole incident still had me extremely uncomfortable.

It was bad enough that Rodney made passes at me but to know that his wife knew about it and that she wanted to be a part of some crazy sex orgy that included the three of us was just disturbing.

It all just made me sick to my stomach.

"Envy?"

I looked up to see that it was Carmen who had interrupted my thoughts.

She had the top down on her black and chromed Mercedes convertible and I must say…she looked like a million bucks.

Unintentionally, I started to wonder if she had once been a *whore-maid* herself, or if she still was.

I wondered how many times she'd given herself to the hotel guests in order to afford such an expensive car.

I was sure that she had.

Or maybe she simply collected a fee from *selling* others.

Whether it was one way or the other, we both knew that a hotel management position didn't pay that damn much; but she wasn't going to add me to the group of women that she made money off of.

She was sadly mistaken.

I just stood there, staring at her as she stared at me.

"Can we talk?"

"I heard you loud and clear yesterday. There's nothing for us to talk about."

"Why are you making this so difficult? I'm trying to help you Envy. Look at you, you need the money," she said, almost sincere.

Seriously?

This woman was really *trying* my patience.

She was about two seconds from a throat punch and she didn't even know it.

Why was it so hard for her to understand that my *precious ruby* didn't come with a price tag?

It was hard enough, for me, to give it up for free.

There was no way in hell that I would be able to try and *sell it*.

I had only been with one man, one time, other than Keymar.

I felt so dirty and guilty that I started to cry while the other man was on top of me.

Keymar had been my first and my only…until that night with the other guy of course. Keymar was the only man I'd ever loved, or even dated for that matter.

As I stated, we'd met in high school and had been joined at the hip ever since.

When he died, we were only three months away from our wedding day.

We really had no excuse as to why we'd taken so long to tie the knot.

We would often say that there was no rush and that we had our whole lives to live and that our best days were ahead of us.

Boy, were we wrong.

But even once he was dead and gone, I still felt extremely loyal to him. I still felt as though I was in a relationship with him although he was no longer with me.

I didn't want to feel that way, but I did.

Even to this day, I did.

Anyway, I tried to force myself to move on.

I tried to force myself to date and move on with my life but it wasn't easy.

But that night, I forced myself to keep going so I allowed my date to *baby step* me through the whole sex thing, but I couldn't wait for it to come to an end.

And that night, I vowed to never put myself in that situation again.

I wasn't giving *it* up, to anyone, until I was ready.

And after three years, I was still unsure as to if I was really ready. Sex with a man or even finding a man were usually the furthest things from my mind.

Sure, I had my lonely nights, and there were plenty of times that I wanted to be touched…inside and out.

But for the most part, I didn't have time to dream or worry about a feeling that could easily be taken care of with my fingers. I was too busy worrying about how to keep my head above water.

Shaking away my thoughts and before I even had a chance to respond to Carmen, the bus turned the corner and in order for them to pull up, Carmen had to pull off.

Glancing in her rearview mirror and without a single word, Carmen sped off without so much as looking back in my direction.

I rolled my eyes and stepped onto the bus.

I didn't need her, her help or her *offer*.

I had options.

After spending hours signing up for benefits, stopping at a few staffing companies, and by the police station, I decided that it was time to head back to my side of town.

It was Wednesday, which was the hotel's payday, so I decided to stop by on my way home.

The hotel wasn't one that had hundreds of different locations all over the world, but it was one that well-known, locally and nationally.

It had been founded by a pretty wealthy family, and it was over one hundred years old.

Honestly, I wasn't sure why they'd never decided to branch out, expand, or start a chain of hotels all over the place.

The hotel was very popular and very successful.

But come to think of it, I'd recently discovered that it was a hotel of many secrets, and I was sure that the secret activities had something to do with keeping things simple.

I guess the one location made sense.

It made it easier to keep things on the *hush.*

I was almost certain that since I was no longer an employee that maybe I was supposed to let them mail my check to me, but I couldn't wait for all of that.

I was already stressing over how I was going to make ends meet and I needed my funds in my hand so that I could accurately calculate everything.

With this check, and the small last three-day check that I would receive next week, Horizon's monthly check and the little assistance that I did get approved for, I figured that I could probably make it for a month or two but after that, I would absolutely have to have a job.

The staffing agencies from earlier promised to submit me to a few open positions, but because of my short list of experiences, I was only promised possible call backs.

But I was hopeful.

Walking into the hotel, immediately, I noticed things that I hadn't noticed before.

I noticed that there were a few maids whom I'd never seen pick up a broom or even push a cart for that matter.

I could only assume that they were a part of the *executive group* of maids as Carmen had called them.

Watching one of the maids that looked out of place, I noticed a married man twisting off his wedding band and then he placed it into his back pocket as he followed the maid towards Carmen's office; instead of heading down the hall to a room or to the lobby elevator.

It's amazing what you see when you're actually *looking*.

I even saw that some of the maids were wearing diamonds, real ones, on their ears, necks and their wrists.

Have you ever known a *maid* to own diamonds?

Nope…me either.

I couldn't believe that I hadn't noticed all of these things before.

How could I have not been paying attention?

And then again, I was always good about minding my own business and protecting my own secrets.

Hiding things seemed to work better when you stayed to yourself.

After standing around for another minute or so, I headed towards Carmen's office.

I was surprised to find that the gentleman and the maid were nowhere in sight once I'd entered.

I hadn't seen them come back out.

Where did they go?

"I'm here for my check," I said without bothering to greet Carmen first.

"What check?"

What the hell did she mean *what check*?

I needed my money and now was not the time to be playing around with my funds.

"Look, we can do this the easy way, or the hard way," I said to her.

She sat back in her chair and smiled.

"Unless you want the police to know about the secret floor, the maid-whores and this little *Hush Hotel* that you are running, I suggest you give me my money."

"You couldn't prove it even if you tried," Carmen said confidently.

"You wanna bet?" I asked her, pulling out my cell phone.

Carmen glared at me.

I could tell that she didn't know whether to believe me or whether she should try to call my bluff but after a while she cleared her throat, reached in her desk and handed me my check.

Bitch.

"It's such a shame. I really liked you too," she said and then lowered her head and pretended to be looking at her paperwork.

The funny thing was that I'd been quite fond of her as well.

Carmen and I had shared good conversations, a few drinks, laughs and even a couple of meals since I'd been working for the hotel.

She had always been so sweet and kind to me.

She had been more than understanding when it came to my babysitting issues and she'd always told me that she would help me in any way that she could.

She'd said that single mothers had a special place in her heart.

Carmen didn't have any kids, but she was one of six kids and she'd said that her mother had always struggled to raise her and her siblings on her own.

From the story that Carmen told me, her mother had killed their father but it had been written off as self-defense; but Carmen had always believed that there was more to the story.

It was clear that Carmen resented her mother's actions but she still admired her for doing everything that she could to raise them and from what she'd said, all but two had made something amazing out of themselves.

But nevertheless, up until Carmen's *indecent proposal*, she'd shown me a ton of compassion.

It was hard for me to believe that she'd given me such an ultimatum in the first place.

But that just goes to show that you never really know a person.

 You just never know what a person has up their sleeve.

Exiting out of the hotel doors, with my check, I attempted to sort out my feelings.

"Oh, excuse me," I said to the gentleman that I'd accidently bumped into without even bothering to look at his face.

"No sweetheart, excuse me," he said behind me, but I didn't bother to look back at him as I started down the street.

As I headed down the busy street, this time instead of worry and grief, I felt a sense of relief.

At that very moment I knew that somehow, someway, things were going to be just fine.

Hopefully.

****

Chapter TWO

"Can I talk to you for a second?" Rodney's wife asked me in a low voice.

I looked at her suspiciously.

I'd seen the police stop by their house a few days ago and her and her husband had been giving me the evil eye ever since.

But I could have cared less.

She was just as sick and stupid as he was.

Against my better judgement, instead of heading into the house, I headed towards her as she stood on her front porch.

I noticed that Rodney's car wasn't there, so I figured that maybe we could talk woman to woman.

"Come on in, have a seat," I walked slowly behind her and sat on the couch.

"Would you like something to drink?"

Yeah…right.

Knowing her she would have probably put something in it.

You just never know with crazy people.

"No thanks. Look, whatever you and Rodney allow to go on in your marriage, that's your business. My only issue is that I would prefer that he keep his comments…and his eyes to himself. I don't have relations with married men and I never will," I explained to her.

She smiled at me.

I never noticed how pretty she was until that moment.

She wasn't black.

I wasn't sure if she was Hispanic or Indian; but she was something.

I was surprised that she'd chosen to be with someone as ugly and unattractive as Rodney.

Maybe she loved him for what was on the inside…and then again, that couldn't be all that much.

Just as she opened her mouth to speak, the front door opened.

Rodney walked in with a smile.

"Good job baby," he said to her and she smiled at him.

What?

What the hell is going on here?

I jumped to my feet but Rodney blocked the door

"Where do you think you are going? The party is just getting started," Rodney said licking his lips.

I turned back to his wife who was slowly backing away from me but she wasn't moving fast enough.

Before I could stop myself, I pounced on her as if I was a cat and she was a mouse.

Obviously, they had some other motives and because of her participation, she was now a lucky recipient of a good ole' Southern style ass whopping!

I don't know what I was thinking coming over here in the first place.

It had been years since I'd been in a physical altercation, but unfortunately for her, it was just like riding a bike.

It seemed as though we had been going at it for forever, but finally Rodney pulled me off his wife.

It wasn't until he had me pinned to the floor that I realized that now he was completely…naked.

What the hell?

When the hell did this fool take off his clothes?

"Get the hell off of me!" I screamed as he held my hands down and pressed his body up against mine.

Out of the corner of my eye, I saw his wife, bleeding… and undressing.

You have got to be kidding me!

Just how crazy are they?

This just could not be happening.

"Rodney, get off of me now! I swear---," but before I could finish my sentence, he kissed me with my mouth still open.

And then he licked me, all the while making some kind of strange noise, all at the same time.

I'd always known that he wasn't right, but this was just sick!

His wife was now assisting him with holding me down as he attempted to peel my clothes off of my squirming body.

I cursed, I screamed, but no one could hear me.

Was I really about to get raped by a husband…and his wife?

I couldn't wrap my mind around it all but I knew that I wasn't going down without a fight.

But thank goodness that I didn't have to fight alone.

The gunshot startled all three of us.

It was Tia.

Where in the hell had she come from?

"If I were you, I would be really careful about what you do next," she said.

She must have found the gun in my top drawer.

"I saw you about to come in the house and then you stopped and came over here. When you didn't come back out and considering what you told me about these two, I assumed that something just wasn't right. I hope you don't mind that I brought a little reinforcement," Tia said and then shot the gun in the wife's direction.

Rodney's wife scream and Tia shot the gun again, just barely missing Rodney's left arm.

Both Rodney and his wife were silent and now on their feet and before I could even get my thoughts together, I hurried off of the floor and ran out the front door.

Saying that I was in shock was an understatement.

I was astonished; flabbergasted even.

I kept running until I was safely inside my house. I saw that Horizon was asleep on the couch so I sat on the couch beside her and covered my mouth as I began to scream.

I couldn't believe that something like that was about to happen to me.

I just couldn't believe it.

My emotions and my mind were all over the place and I began to cry tears of disbelief and anger.

Seconds later, the front door opened and Tia appeared.

She was carrying my gun and my purse.

"Are you okay?"

I jumped to my feet and embraced her.

I cried on her shoulder and she held me close to her.

She didn't say a word for a while and then she instructed me that we needed to call the police.

A little while later, the police arrived but no justice was served.

Rodney and his wife were gone.

And I was sure that they would never be coming back.

"Thank you for today. I can't even imagine what would have happened if you hadn't showed up when you did," I said to Tia later on that night.

I was still slightly freaked out, so she and Horizon were both sleeping in the bed with me.

"No thanks needed. You are my sister and I am my sister's keeper. I'm just glad that I had been looking out the window otherwise I would have never seen you go over there," she said to me with a frown.

We small talked about the situation for a little while longer and then Tia fell asleep.

She'd saved my life and she didn't even know it.

And little did she know, once before, I'd saved hers too.

***

"Mommy, I'm hot," my daughter managed to say.

The air conditioning unit stopped working a few days ago, and we were miserable.

We had fans, but they just didn't seem to be getting the job done.

It was barely the middle of summer, and during the day, without air conditioning, all the fans seemed to do was blow in hot air.

I'd had someone come out to take a look at the unit and of course, it was old and needed to be replaced.

It was one of the few things that we hadn't upgraded when we'd started remodeling the house.

I remembered mentioning it to Keymar but he assured me that it was in pretty good condition so he thought that it was best that we wait to replace it.

I guess he had been wrong.

Since the incident, a while ago with the crazy neighbors, I'd been thinking of Keymar a lot.

Had he been there, something like that would have never happened in the first place.

He would have been there to protect me.

Though strangely he still had my heart, I was starting to see the value in moving on and letting go.

People were crazy these days and sadly a single mother with no man around made me an easy target.

And I would surely kill somebody if I ever even came close to going through something like that again.

The police had yet to find Rodney and his wife and I was sure that they were long gone and probably in a different state by now.

I was one tough cookie so the shock of it all was over but the anger wasn't going anywhere anytime soon.

For their sake, they'd better hope that I never, ever saw them again.

Anyway, to repair the air conditioning unit, it was going to be hundreds of dollars that I just didn't have.

I'd made a couple of trips to the nearest pawn shop to see if they had a used, cheap, window air conditioning unit, but so far, I hadn't had much luck.

I just couldn't afford to buy a brand new one.

I had to budget and save what little money I had left.

It was coming up on the fourth week since I'd lost my job at the hotel and I was starting to feel the pressure.

My unemployment had yet to be approved.

It appears as though I called them every other day to check on the status, but I was always told that it could take anywhere from eight to twelve weeks.

Who in the hell could wait up to twelve weeks for unemployment?

The point of filing it in the first place was because a person was now *unemployed*, which meant that they no longer had a damn job!

Who in the hell made that rule?

Whosever bright idea it was to make anyone in a horrible situation, wait that long for what was rightfully theirs should be slapped in the face, twice, with the back side of a sixty-year-old grandma's hand.

Seriously, with such a long waiting period, a person could be homeless and hungry by then; especially with how hard it was to find a job these days.

Speaking of, I hadn't received one single call back and to date I'd probably put in at least a hundred applications.

I'd even applied for other maid positions, but as of yet, nothing.

Though I tried to hide it, I was stressed to death.

I was so worried about the next day and bills that I had to drug myself up on medication at night just to get a decent night's rest.

And being jobless, soon to be homeless and addicted to pain medication was one hell of a bad combination.

So, something had to change and it had better change fast!

My sister, Tia, entered the living room as I began to strip my daughter down to cool her off.

Tia was wearing only a t-shirt that barely covered the bottom of her *panty-less* ass.

She flopped down on the sofa across from me.

"I can get you the money to fix the air," she said nonchalantly.

I eyed her suspiciously.

My daughter, now down to just her underwear, took off running and I waited for Tia to speak.

In my opinion, Tia was the most attractive of all of the sisters.

She was a dark, mysterious complexion.

I'm talking about as dark as midnight or so dark that it was difficult to see her if all of the lights were off.

Yes, I know that some may think that dark skinned women weren't the prettiest, but she was one of the most beautiful women I'd ever seen.

She was flawless, stunning, even if she didn't have on a stitch of make-up.

Tia in a way reminded me of a black Chinese woman. It was a weird comparison, but it was just something about the shape of her eyes and the structure of her face. But she also possessed the high cheek bones, full lips, and dominating smile of a sista', all day, every day.

She was truly a sight to see.

"I have a friend. I can ask him for the money," she said.

Immediately I shook my head no.

"It's okay, I'll figure it out. There's no telling what you will have to do for your *friend*, just to get it. I'll figure out something," I said to her and got up from the chair, signaling that the conversation was over.

She didn't say another word, she simply started to hum.

I wasn't selling my body and I surely wasn't going to allow my baby sister to sell hers.

There just had to be another way.

***

"Where have you been?" I asked Tia as she tip-toed into the house.

It was two o'clock in the morning and I'd been waiting for her since about ten.

I'd dozed off while I was reading Horizon a bedtime story and when I woke up, Tia was nowhere to be found and she wasn't answering her cell phone.

"Last time I checked I was grown you know," she responded with an attitude.

She entered the living room, barefooted.

She dropped her shoes from her hands to the floor beside the table, exhaled and then she laid on the couch and closed her eyes.

I could smell the alcohol on her.

I was just a little jealous because she'd gotten drunk without me. I was the one that needed a drink.

But my money was so *funny* that I would even hesitate spending a few dollars on a bottle of wine out of fear that I might need the money for something else.

The struggle was real.

"Oh, I almost forgot," Tia said and reached into her bra.

She pulled out a wad of cash and threw it in my direction.

"Here you go. It's $1000. That should be, enough right? Oh, and you're welcome," she said and turned her back to me.

Immediately I began to question her about the money but she didn't give me a single response.

The only answer I received was the sound of her light snores.

Hesitantly, I picked up the money and proceeded to count it.

I could only hope that she hadn't had to do anything that she would regret just to help me.

I was supposed to be helping her, yet here lately she was the one coming through for me.

I retrieved a blanket and placed it over her.

Kissing her forehead, I mumbled the words *thank you* and headed to bed.

I sat the money on the night stand, undressed and forced myself to relax.

And surprisingly, that night, for the first time in forever, and without any medication, I fell asleep just fine.

The next morning, as soon as I opened my eyes, I made a few calls to a few people and finally a family friend of ours agreed to fix the unit for about eight hundred dollars.

"I know you have spent the last hour or so making calls, but I have a suggestion. Go and buy two window units; one for the front of the house and one for the back. It's a lot cheaper, and that way you can use the rest of the money for other things. Those two units should cool the house just fine. Not to mention we can keep on a fan or two. And you won't have to spend but a hundred, or two at the most," Tia suggested.

She was right.

I could get the old central unit replaced some other time and the extra money would help tremendously.

And since it was Tia who had brought the money home, so to speak, it was only right to do as she said with it.

After getting a cousin of ours to take us to get the window air conditioners, and once the house started to cool off, I headed to the kitchen to start dinner.

As I watched Tia play with Horizon, I couldn't help but reminisce about Tia when she was her age.

We were many years apart in age, but I could remember watching after her and pretending as if she was my own child.

With Mama being a school teacher and all back then, she seemed to be so busy teaching other people's kids, that it somewhat fell on my shoulders to teach my siblings what she'd taught me; especially when it came to Tia.

I taught Tia her ABC's and how to tie her shoes. I was the one that taught her how to ride her bike and I'd even been the one to teach her how to read.

Minus the child birth and labor pains, I was pretty much who she looked at as Mama and I was the first one that she came to when she needed help or answers.

I was who she wanted to tuck her in at night.

It was me who tended to her bruises and I was the one to rescue her from the monsters that lived under her bed.

I was also the one who saved her from Uncle Johnnie.

Uncle Johnnie was Mama's adopted brother.

Well, I don't even think he was adopted…legally.

His parents had died when he was in his teens and my grandparents had taken him in.

But real uncle or not, he was the biggest drunk that I'd ever seen and nobody seemed to care that he was drinking his life away.

But I hated him…especially when he was drunk.

He was always too touchy-feely if you ask me but no one else seemed to notice.

But I did…I noticed.

I would always watch him and how he would look at all of us, especially Tia.

She was only about four at the time, but I remembered coming into the house from playing outside to find her. I'd noticed that I hadn't seen her for a while and I'd gone to look for her.

As soon as I entered the house, I'd heard him trying to bribe Tia with candy to follow him into the back room.

When I turned the corner to the hallway I could see that his pants were already undone and that his penis was already as hard as a rock.

Nasty bastard!

Luckily, I'd come into the house, just in time, before things had gone too far but for me, he'd gone far enough.

I looked at him with disgust as he tried to look innocent and attempted to pull himself together.

I grabbed Tia's hand and led her back outside with me. I was so furious that day that I began to cry.

Why couldn't anyone else see how unstable and sick he was?

Why didn't anyone else care that he had a problem and that he had a thing for little girls?

It was as clear as day yet everyone acted as though there was nothing wrong.

As I allowed Tia to get back to playing on that sunny day, I'd dried my eyes and began to brainstorm.

He had to pay for what he'd tried to do to my little sister. He had to be stopped or else he would have tried it again and who knows, he probably would've succeeded if I hadn't done what I did.

To this day, I often forgot about what I'd done and usually kept it buried in the pit of my belly where no one would ever find out the truth.

It was one of the many secrets that I had but nowhere near one of the worst.

What I'd done was something that I wasn't proud of but I had to stop him.

I couldn't let him hurt Tia, so I did what I thought was right at the time.

That's right…I cried wolf.

I waited for about a week after the incident.

During that time, I'd explored my vagina and used anything I could to widen it, stretch and enter it to look as though I'd been *touched* before.

Once Mama left us home alone with Uncle Johnnie one evening, I knew that I had to make my move.

I almost decided not to go through with it until I saw him touch himself as he watched Tia and one of our other sisters as they played.

I knew then that he deserved to be in jail and it was up to me to put him there.

So, the next morning, I started acting weird and when Mama asked me what was wrong, I lied.

I told her that Uncle Johnnie had touched me the day before and had been touching me for years.

I was sure to say that the day before he'd only fondled me but I expressed that he'd done everything else on other occasions.

I forced myself to cry and even gave vivid details, as best as I could.

The internet had been my only resource, but apparently, it was enough.

I know, I know, it wasn't right.

And I was too young to tell such a drastic lie but I felt as though it was my only option.

I had to do something.

Maybe I could have simply told Mama the truth about the way that he looked at Tia and maybe she would have kept him away from her.

But would that have been enough?

What if he tried to hurt someone else?

He had a ton of kids by a lot of different women all over the place, some of which we'd never even met.

What if he touched one of them?

If I wasn't mistaken most of them were girls, so, in my mind, that made them possible victims.

But nevertheless, the saddest part of all was that my lie actually worked.

I stuck to my story, and lied until Uncle Johnnie was convicted of a crime that he didn't do.

He called me liar after liar but no one believed him.

Everyone believed me.

Mama, the police department, the judge and the jury all believed me.

Because of my allegations, Uncle Johnnie received a few years in prison.

I figured that by the time he got out, Tia would at least be old enough to defend herself, but Uncle Johnnie never came back home.

He died only three months after going to prison of some widespread prison viral outbreak that he'd contracted.

Did I feel bad?

Heck yeah, I did.

I never meant for him to die.

I was just trying to save my sister.

If I could do everything all over again, I wouldn't have told such an awful lie, instead, I would have told the truth but I couldn't change it.

And it was something that I'd had to deal with my whole life.

It was a guilt that had never, ever gone away.

But whenever I looked at Tia, and all of her accomplishments, for the most part, I felt as though I'd saved her life.

Who knows where she would have been if he had gotten ahold of her.

Who knows how she would have turned out or if she would have even made it to where she was today if he had stolen her innocence.

I knew that one day I would be held accountable for what I'd done, but at the time, as a young naïve little girl, my heart was in the right place.

And for my sanity, I had to believe that my actions had resulted in something good.

It was just one of those things that you never told a soul and I was taking the truth, and such a big secret with me to my grave.

Point. Blank. Period.

Shaking away the thoughts of my past, I focused back on my current life and current situation.

I had to find a job and I had to find one fast!

There weren't a lot of folks that I could depend on and I couldn't have Tia doing other things to lighten my load.

Though we had two other sisters, Sonni and Josephine, they were both married with a ton of kids so I never reached out to them for any type of assistance.

Even if they did have it to spare, I just didn't feel right asking them for anything.

So, I had to fix my situation on my own, just as I always had before.

Though I didn't want to think about what Tia had to do for the money, the extra money was definitely going to pay a few bills that needed to be taken care of.

But that money would also run out and I had to have something in the works by then.

I started to think about my options.

Are there any opportunities that I was overlooking?

If my car was fixed, I could get something as simple as a paper route.

They were always hiring and you didn't need any education or experience to throw a newspaper at a house.

I knew plenty of folks that made a living out of delivering newspapers for two to three hours a night, seven days a week.

But you had to have a reliable or at least a working car for that.

I already knew that finding someone to fix the transmission in the car was going to be very expensive and I was sure that it would take every penny that I had left.

So, the whole newspaper delivery idea was out the window.

I dropped a piece of chicken into the hot grease and sat down in a chair in front of the stove.

There had to be something that I could do.

"Envy! Look!" Tia yelled.

I hurried to the living room and followed Tia's eyes to the television.

There they were, Rodney and his wife, on the news.

They'd been pulled over somewhere in Georgia and instead of surrendering; they led the police on a high-speed chase.

Unfortunately, for them, the chase ended in their deaths.

Rodney lost control of the car and the car flipped over several times before bursting into flames.

They were both pronounced dead at the scene.

Though they'd tried to hurt me, I did feel just a small bit of sympathy but it didn't last long.

I'm sorry…but that's two less sick minded people on this planet.

And I was all for getting rid of a sick-minded person.

And my past could vouch for that.

***

"What's wrong with you Tia?" I asked her as she leaned over the toilet to throw up again.

She'd been packing her things to head back to campus and suddenly, she took off running to the bathroom.

Her summer vacation was officially over and it was time for her to get back to her studies.

She went to a local university, but she was on a full scholarship that included housing.

I'd watched her work her tail off to get her education and I would do anything in the world to make sure that she made it across that stage.

"I'm pregnant Envy," she said in between gags.

Pregnant?

What the hell did she mean she was pregnant?

"Tia, what do you mean you're pregnant? Why aren't you on birth control? How could you be so stupid?" I screamed at her in disappointment.

She gave me a look that could kill.

"First of all, I was, am, on the pill so I have no idea how this could have happened. Secondly, I only had sex once in the past six months…to get you the money for the air conditioners. So, sorry, for being stupid as you said. I was only trying to help," Tia growled and pushed her way out of the bathroom.

I sat on the edge of the tub and thought about what she'd said.

My struggling had ruined my baby sister's life.

Don't get me wrong, children are blessings from above, but she had so much potential and so many goals and a baby was only going to slow her down.

There was just no way she could have this baby.

She was almost to the finish line and I just couldn't let her ruin her life.

After thinking a little while longer, I got up to go and find Tia.

She was sitting on the edge of the bed in the room that used to be our parents.

Though it was the biggest bedroom in the house, I'd turned it into a guest bedroom.

I simply couldn't sleep in a room that reminded me so much of Mama and Daddy.

But Tia never seemed to have a problem with it.

"I'm sorry," I said to her.

"It's okay. I shouldn't have opened my legs to him anyway. After all he was my professor…last year…and not to mention that he's married," Tia said.

I looked at her in disbelief.

"Why would you do something like that Tia?"

"You needed the money. Horizon needed the money. And I knew that he would give it to me. He'd made passes at me all year and he'd offered me everything except a Rolls Royce to get inside of my pants. I asked him for the money and he said yes with no problem. I just knew that I would have to do something in return. That's just the way that it is. That's just the way that this world works. Everyone wants something. But I don't understand how I got pregnant. I take my pills faithfully. I should not be pregnant but unfortunately, I am. And yes, I told him. He told me that he would pay for the abortion, but I think I'm going to keep it," she said.

I was surprised at her response.

Why would she want to keep a baby by a married man?

It just didn't seem fair to the baby.

I'd had an abortion when I was just seventeen years old.

It was another one of my secrets that no one other than my cousin that paid for it, knew about.

Yes, it was by Keymar, but I wasn't ready to be a mother.

I thought that I wanted to do other things after high school and I thought that I was going to have this full and busy life and I thought a baby was going to slow me down.

Funny thing was, it was Keymar who'd called all of the shots, so I hadn't ended up doing any of the things that I thought I was going to do.

Nevertheless, I told my older cousin my secret, and she'd taken me to take care of it.

We never told anyone, not even Keymar, and it was another one of those secrets that I had in my closet full of skeletons.

If Mama had known what I'd done she would have surely killed me, but at the time, I thought that I was doing what was best for me.

"Tia, you have to be smart about this. He's married, and offering to pay for an abortion which means that you will be doing this all on your own if you keep this baby. Do you really want to do that? Look at me. It's not easy. And what about school?"

"I know, it seems crazy, but I can do it. I don't need him and I won't even bother him. This is the consequence of my actions and I'm going to deal with it even though I'll have to deal with it on my own. I'm still going to go to school but I was wondering if I could stay here and just go to campus on the days that I have classes. I can work my class schedule around and still help you watch Horizon when you get a new job. I'm going to need you to help me get through this and I'm going to be here to help you. All we have is each other. By the time the baby is due, I'll be almost finished. I will graduate this year and I will find a good job and take care of my baby," Tia said confidently.

Her confidence reminded me so much of Mama.

Mama had been a strong, smart black woman.

She was the definition of strength, dedication and hard work.

Mama was the kind of woman that could turn a dime into a dollar. She could turn one pack of meat, flour, two can goods, and milk into a buffet.

She had been our very own, real life super woman and Tia reminded me so much of her.

Internally, I couldn't help but blame myself for the situation.

Had it not been because of me she wouldn't have given herself to a married man and she wouldn't be carrying his baby.

I had been the one dumb enough to sit around and wait on a man to take care of me, instead of at least getting a higher education and making something of myself.

I was the one that didn't have anything to offer.

I was the one who couldn't find a decent job.

I was the one struggling.

It was me…not her.

But that was all going to change.

And it was going to change today.

The next few hours came with planning and preparation.

Tia was officially going to stay in the house with me and commute to school for her classes.

Her best friend vowed to get her back and forth on the days that she had classes and Tia promised me that she was going to work her ass off, pregnant and all, to graduate at the top of her class…on time.

After she and Horizon were down for a nap, I headed out the door to do something that I should have done a long time ago.

I was going to beg Carmen for my job back at the hotel.

With Tia being pregnant, I was going to have to make sure that she was comfortable and taken care of especially since it was my fault that she was in the predicament that she was in.

I just had to put my pride aside and do what was best for my family…even if it was going to make me uncomfortable.

What other choice did I have?

Maybe Carmen would see how much I needed the job and help me out.

I could only hope that she would do the right thing.

Please let her have the heart of the caring, generous woman that I'd met two years ago because I really, really, needed a job.

I walked into the hotel and a feeling of discomfort smacked me dead in the face.

Immediately, I felt as though I was walking from a prison cell, heading towards my own execution.

But thoughts of Horizon, Tia, and the unborn baby kept my feet moving until I reached Carmen's office.

I knocked and she looked up at me.

Shockingly, she didn't seem surprised to see me.

It was as though she had been expecting me.

"Envy, what a surprise," she said although I knew that she was lying.

I wasn't a fan of begging but I was all out of options.

"I need my job back Carmen," I said to her hesitantly.

I wondered if maybe I should cry or at least shed a tear to pull at the strings of her heart.

I really, really needed my job back, so I opened my mouth to say a few more words.

"I know things went kind of sour, but I really need a job. I've looked everywhere and I haven't had any luck. Even if it's for fewer hours, whatever, I just really need my job back," I said to her.

I felt like the scum of the earth to have to beg her but my pride was the last thing that I was worried about.

I had people to take care of.

I had people depending on me.

Carmen was quiet.

She looked at me with pity, yet it seemed like she'd enjoyed hearing me beg.

Forcing herself not to smile, so she spoke instead.

"I'm sorry Envy, but your position was filled a long time ago," she said.

I exhaled.

What was I doing here anyway?

I should have known better than to come here.

I didn't say a word. I simply turned around to leave.

"But---I am still hiring for another position," Carmen said behind me.

How did I know that it would come to this?

"You see, I saved a spot just for you on our *team*, you know, just in case you changed your mind," she said.

I turned around to face her.

My mind was racing and I was confused as to what to do.

How on earth was I going to give my most prized possession to men that I didn't know?

How would I get through it all without being sick to my stomach?

Especially with the incident that Rodney and his wife had recently put me through.

Being violated was not a good feeling.

But what other options did I have?

I had a family to take care of and I needed a job.

I was almost out of money and I was all out of time.

From the looks of it, this was the only option that I had left.

I mean, maybe it wasn't all that bad.

Maybe I could at least see what the *job* really consisted of.

Maybe I could try it out or at least try to do it for a month or two, just to get back on my feet.

Yes, there was a little light at the end of this dark tunnel.

If the *job* paid as well as Carmen had said, I would be on my feet in no time and I would have saved up enough money to take care of home until something better came along.

This was the only way.

As sad as it was, this was my only option.

"Okay, I will do it. But under one condition," I said to her.

"You're not really in a situation to make any demands, but proceed," Carmen said, standing up and walking towards me.

"No married men. I don't care if they *request* me as you said or whatever. I absolutely will not sleep with a married man," I said to her.

She smiled at me.

"Honey, half of the time we don't know what they have at home. We have a "don't ask don't tell" policy. That is unless they're a governor or big time celebrity or something. We have a lot of those types of men as *clients*. And so of course we know all about their family lives. But when it comes to the real money makers, sometimes we hardly know anything about their personal lives. But I'll try my best. You have morals. So, you have my word. But just so you know, married men usually pay the most," she said, closing and locking her office door and then she reached for my hand.

I was skeptical, but I took a deep breath and took it.

We walked to the back of the office and she pressed firmly up against the wall.

The wall opened and I saw an elevator.

Well, I'll be...

This bitch had a secret elevator behind a wall in her office and I was guessing that the elevator led up to the secret, hidden floor.

We stepped on the elevator and I became extremely nervous as the doors closed and we started to move.

Only seconds later, the elevator doors opened and there it was.

The thirteenth floor.

I couldn't believe my eyes.

I mean it didn't look a thing like the other twelve floors of the hotel.

Sure, the hotel was nice, but it looked like any other hotel to me.

But here, on the thirteenth floor, it was very elegant, to say the least.

It was exquisitely decorated.

It looked like the top floor of a mansion or the cover page of a magazine.

It was a sight to see and so were the women.

Some of the maids on the floor, I'd never even seen before.

Some of them were drop dead gorgeous and most of them were extremely fit.

They looked like super models, well if you add an extra twenty-five pounds in all of the right places.

But none of them were as shapely as I was and they didn't have anything near my curves; which made me feel extremely out of place.

Most of the maids were topless, and only wore the bottom half of maid outfits; very sexy, risqué, bottom halves of maid outfits.

Other maids didn't have on maid outfits at all.

They were completely naked except for diamonds, six-inch pumps, and maid headwear.

At the sight of Carmen, all of the women smiled and disappeared into different rooms.

I counted a total of eight ladies but I could only assume that there were more.

Passing by the rooms, I saw that all of them ended in the number 13.

Envy, you still have time to walk away from this.

My heart was trying to talk me out of it all but my mind was curious.

So, despite that it was a lot to take in and I was a tad bit sick to my stomach, I followed Carmen anyway.

I was surprised at the fresh scent of flowers and other aromas in the air.

Considering all of the bare ass that had been walking up and down the hallway, it smelled rather refreshing.

Soon, Carmen and I entered a room.

It looked like a lounge, and a boutique mixed together.

There were maid uniforms of a few different colors; some were even leopard or zebra print.

But it was mostly just the bottoms.

There were either no tops or lace bras of the same color on the top half of the hangers.

There were high priced shoes, with price tags still on to them.

Gucci, Louis Vuitton, you name it, it was there.

I saw different types of expensive fragrances, diamond earrings, along with whips, chains and handcuffs.

There were also cleaning supplies, bottles of champagne and even expensive lace front wigs.

All I could think to myself was…wow.

"Everything that you see, you can use or have. We get a new shipment of the latest once a month. What's here is what's left from this month. If it's your size or if you like it, you simply take it with you. You can have it," Carmen said.

Was she serious?

All of this expensive stuff was free?

Well, free might be putting a little too much on it.

After all you were selling your ass and throwing away your morals and respect, so they might as well shower you with material things.

We continued through the room and came to another hallway.

As we headed down it, I saw bathrooms that looked as though they didn't belong in hotels.

One for the maids and one for the guests.

Both were full of expensive tile, glass showers and big soaker tubs.

Walking on, I even saw a small gym.

And Carmen mentioned that there was also another hallway of rooms, which were the guest's actual *sleeping* quarters.

To be honest, I couldn't believe my eyes.

I'd worked at the bottom for two whole years.

Never would I have imagined that all of this was taking place right above my head.

In another room, there was a desk that Carmen took a seat behind.

I sat down in front of her.

Get up, and get out of here Envy. This is your last chance.

My conscious started to kick in but I still didn't move.

I just sat there.

After a while, Carmen handed me a stack of papers.

"What's this?" I asked her.

"It's an application---slash contract silly. I know you didn't think that you wouldn't have to sign a contract. And of course, the application is to rehire you as a "maid". Though you won't be doing any *regular* maid duties; it's just so that everything looks legit. And might I add that on top of what you receive up here, you'll still get a paycheck as if you were cleaning up just like others downstairs. I told you this position comes with a lot of perks. So, you're getting a *regular* paycheck though you aren't a *regular* maid anymore. Well, I mean, you will be responsible for cleaning your *room*; but that's it. You will still be *on* four days and off for three; just as you were before. The contract states that if you accept to become an *executive* maid, you are bound to the duties for at least one year. This means, you can't walk away from it for a whole 365 days that you sign your name on the dotted line. If you do, you will owe all of the money that you made while on the thirteenth floor as well as returning all of the items you take or use from our monthly supply. If you have used it or worn the items, you are then responsible for the total value of the item. Doesn't seem like we can do this considering the type of business that this is? Trust me, we can. You see, of course I'm not the head of this operation. No, the head is a judge, a district attorney, a captain of a police station, as well as an attorney and a celebrity or two. Where do you think our clientele comes from? So, if you think of quitting, you will be bound by the contract and either you pay back every dime that you earned or you will have to deal with the consequences. And if you try to tell and bring down the operation, we keep a record of everything you do and all of the men that you screw. So, remember that you could possibly face criminal charges as well. Prostitution is a crime. Not to mention that all our clients and executive maids will deny your claims. And I'm sure the police department will *accidently lose* your report anyway before it gets to that point, but I still have to tell you these things. Just so you have an idea of the type of "power" you are dealing with. There are some powerful people and names involved with this and trust me, you don't want to cross them. Who knows, you could even end up…dead or something. I'm just keeping it real. So, I have to ask you Envy…are you sure?" Carmen said, extending a pen in my direction.

She'd said a mouth full!

She went on to explain how the process worked and how the clients *ordered* the woman that they wanted to entertain them while in town for business or whatever the reason was that they were staying at the hotel.

She also explained how the payment process worked. Payments were made in all cash. The price was tailored to whatever service they ordered. It was like room service; except that *ass* was on the menu.

As well as oral sex and other things that I'd never even heard of.

But it all came with a price…a fairly expensive price.

She said that the *maids* usually made half of what the client paid for the services and that whatever the client gave to the maid as a *tip* she could keep it in full.

Carmen also stated that I would be assigned to a room. It would be my own personal room and the only room that I used to *entertain*.

I would be responsible for cleaning it after each sexual encounter and she even suggested that I decorated it or set it up in a way that made the *guests* or clients a little more comfortable.

She expressed that she would be the only other person, other than myself, with a room key and that on occasions, before I arrived at the hotel, there may be a client already waiting for me.

My room would only be used for whatever they purchased. After we were done, the guest, or client, if he was staying overnight, would have a room just for sleeping on the other side of the floor.

I sat in disbelief.

It was so much to take in, and I wasn't sure if I was going to be able to do it.

I wasn't sure if I was going to be able to have sex for money and for a whole year?

That was just down right foolish!

I mean, a year was entirely too long.

It just didn't seem practical.

I'd planned just to get on my feet, but a whole year was asking for way too much.

There was no telling how many dicks would have been in *my Gina's mouth*, or even in my mouth for that matter.

Oh, hell no!

This just isn't for me.

I knew deep down in my heart that this wasn't the right thing for me to do.

I could feel it in my gut. I could feel it in my bones.

As soon as I thought about my health, it was as if Carmen had read my mind.

She explained that a few doctors were on board as well and that the maids were tested once every month, and that the men had to have seen one of these doctors within a month, prior to coming to the hotel for *services.*

But she also said that they required that all of the maids use protection but at the end of the day grown men and women were going to do what they wanted to do.

They had it all figured out but I still didn't think that this was the right move for a woman like me.

I wasn't this type of woman.

But if I walked away right now, and if I didn't find a job in the next week or so, my daughter, my pregnant sister, and I would soon be out on the street.

I had to do something.

This was my last resort.

I tried to figure out what else I could do, but I didn't have any other options.

After about ten more minutes of listening to Carmen talk and trying to convince myself to walk away, I took the pen from her hand.

I hesitated for a while but when a text message came to my phone from Tia stating that the water had been shut off, that was the last straw.

Hurriedly, I signed my name on the dotted line.

For the most part, I felt as though I'd just sold my soul to the Devil or something.

I couldn't believe that I was going to do this.

I was still unsure as to whether or not I was actually going to be able to actually do it, but I had to do something.

I was sure that this was going to be the longest year of my life but I had to do something to help my family.

If Mama was looking down on me, she was surely frowning and shaking her head, but this was the hand that life had dealt me and this was a temporary fix to a temporary situation.

I was going to save every dollar that I could and I was even going to enroll into school in the meantime so that I would never have to settle for something like this again.

Yes, I could see this pushing me in the direction that I should have been going in a long time ago.

After taking a semi-nude picture for the *booty menu*, and receiving another regular maid uniform and name tag that I was supposed to wear into the hotel until I was on the thirteenth floor to change, Carmen lead me back to the secret elevator and back down to her regular office.

Silently, I headed for the door but just as I turned the knob, Carmen called my name.

"Oh, Envy, I almost forgot," she said as she reached me an envelope from her file cabinet.

"Here's your key. You will be using Room 313. For a year, or however long you decide to be with us, this will be the only room that you use. Whatever you do in that room stays in that room. I'm sure you understand the importance of keeping your mouth closed. Our clients trust that things will always remain discreet; so that means, don't say a word, to anyone, about anything you do on the thirteenth floor. Also, in here is your sign-on bonus," she said and watched me open the envelope.

"It's $2,500. Enjoy your day Envy," she said and turned her back to me.

I headed out the door and I didn't stop or even look up until I was out of the hotel and back out on the street

Did all of that really just happen?

Was I really about to become a maid-whore?

With my mind all over the place, I walked home slowly.

The whole thing came with so many problems.

I was already so uncomfortable being touched so I didn't have a clue as to how I was going to get through it all.

Carmen explained that I may not have to have sex with a random man every single day that I was *so-called* at work.

It was only if I was *ordered*.

But she did specify that I could be ordered multiple times a day, but no more than three times.

Three different men in one day?

Oh, I definitely wouldn't be able to do that.

I was hoping that most of the *clients* preferred the tooth-pick skinny girls more so than a woman with curves.

Carmen had already mentioned that she was going to have to custom order some of the sexier bottoms to fit my hips, so it was obvious that curves weren't the normal.

Maybe being plus-sized in this situation was a good thing.

Yeah, maybe I would rarely be ordered.

The good thing was that either way I still got a paycheck.

So, I still would have a little something coming in and that was more than having nothing coming in at all.

My thoughts consumed me but no matter what I thought, I'd already signed the papers.

But I haven't spent any of the money yet, or officially started so I could go back and give everything back and tell her I changed my mind.

I would still be within the terms of the contract and I could just go on.

I can't do this.

What was I thinking?

Just as I'd made my decision, Carmen flew down the road, beeping her horn at me just as I was about to turn back around and head towards the hotel.

You have got to be kidding me!

Well, so much for that plan.

I turned back around and continued to head towards my house instead.

Arriving only a few minutes later, I checked the mail but I didn't look through any of it right off, instead I just sat on the top step and just thought about everything that was about to happen.

I wouldn't be able to tell a soul, but that wouldn't be all that difficult for me to do.

This was another one of those things that I would have to take with me to my grave.

I would tell Tia that I got my job back but that I was now the head maid or office manager so that she wouldn't question me too much about the extra money.

Since she was going to be around a lot more often, I would have to spend lightly, even if I had plenty.

I didn't plan on spending too much anyway since my primary goal was to save.

As soon as my year was up, I was getting as far away from that place as I possibly could.

I would never utter a single word about anything that I did or said in that place.

Everything that I did in that hotel from this point on would be one big secret.

I told myself that once I walked out of there, I would leave my regrets and shame behind me, and pretend as though none of it ever happened.

That was the only way that I was going to mentally be able to get through this.

That was the only way I was going to be able to face myself in the mirror every day.

I took a deep breath and I pulled the envelope full of money and my room key from my purse just to look at it again.

I hadn't seen this much money in such a long time.

I mean, Mama left behind a few thousands when she passed away but I hadn't really handled the money then.

When Keymar was alive he handled all of the money, all of the time and since he had been gone, I'd been lucky to see five hundred dollars at a time, let alone twenty-five hundred dollars.

I placed the envelope of money back inside my purse and looked through the stack of bills.

For the first time, ever, I didn't feel depressed or overwhelmed.

For the first time, ever, I wasn't worried or scared of what might happen.

For the first time, ever, I had more than enough money to cover them, all of them, and I had to admit…it felt damn good.

Looking at the last envelope, my eyes became as big as golf balls as I noticed that it wasn't a bill at all.

I opened it in a hurry and shook my head.

It was my unemployment…and I'd been approved.

Really?

On the day that I'd given in and decided to sell my soul and my body, my unemployment finally comes through?

This is some straight bull!

I looked at the amount and surprisingly I laughed aloud.

What was I supposed to do with this?

Sure, had it not been for the $2,500 of *hush money* sitting snuggly in my purse maybe I would have been a little more grateful.

But for whatever reason, at that moment, I found it hard to be appreciative.

This world was designed to keep us down, so it was up to me to pull myself up.

And I was going to do it the only way that I knew how.

Tearing up the approval letter, I was agreeing to give my life and my body to the hotel and as hard as it was, to get my life on the right track, I knew that it was the best thing for me to do.

But I was only in it for the money…and I was going to make that crystal clear.

****

Chapter THREE

Envy you're late. Follow me, I need you to come chat with me for a second," Carmen said.

I'd only been on the thirteenth floor for about a week and so far, I hadn't been *ordered*.

So, for the four days a week that I was required to *work*, I'd just sat around in my *room* and done nothing.

I hadn't bothered fixing up.

To me, fixing it up would suggest that I was comfortable and that was the last thing that I was.

It was already a nice room; nicer than the rooms on the floors below.

And adding to it or making it as though I was here to stay was pointless.

I'd passed by some of the other rooms and saw that most of them were rather lavish; but the standard look to me was just fine.

It didn't matter what I put in the room; it wouldn't change the fact of what I had to do while in the room.

Since taking the *position*, I'd signed up for online classes to become a medical assistant.

I figured that by the time my year was up at the hotel, I would be certified, and I was sure that finding a new job would be a piece of cake.

So far, I hadn't become too acquainted with any of the other women on the floor.

And honestly, I didn't really plan to.

Actually, none of the women were all that friendly with each other. You hardly ever heard a whole bunch of chatting and I rarely saw any of them really engaging with each other or even mingling in the common areas.

You saw it some…but not too much.

It wasn't like I thought it was going to be.

It was as though all of the women were there to do their dirty deeds, make their money and go home.

And that was just fine with me.

Finally, Carmen and I made it to her upstairs office and we both took a seat.

"So, Envy, you've been *ordered*," Carmen said.

My heart immediately felt as though it'd fallen out of my chest into the pit of my stomach.

"Now, the good news is that he isn't married. Just like you wanted," Carmen said.

I let out a deep breath.

At least she was sticking to her word on that one.

Slut maid or not, there were some standards and some things that I just wouldn't do and I was not going to screw someone else's husband.

"Now, I wanted to talk to you because this is your first time and…"

Oh, no, I didn't like the sound of this.

"He ordered what we called the *Brown Sugar Boom*; which means he wants the works. He wants to be able to do whatever he wants to do to you. And he wants the same in return. Meaning vaginal and oral sex, possibly, and who knows what else. Basically, he wants to get his freak on. Now since you are new, I was hoping that your first time would be something simple or basic, but there's nothing that I can do except deliver you as he requested. He's already here. And I've already placed him in your room. He's been waiting for a few minutes, so we have to wrap this up so that we can get you ready. Your cut will be a little over three thousand dollars plus whatever he tips you; and he is a regular and a very good tipper. He's a billionaire. He has more money than he, his children and even his children's children will be able to spend in their lifetime. But there is something else that you should know," Carmen said.

I was already feeling dirty, and not in a good way, and I hadn't even done anything yet.

And I was sure that whatever she was going to say next wasn't going to make me feel any better.

"He's almost 70 years old."

Did she say 70?

As in seven decades?

Ugh…how gross!

First of all, his old ass needed to sit down somewhere and go roll around in a wheel chair or something.

He was supposed to be somewhere praying and preparing to die. He had no business at a hotel, trying to get a piece of ass!

There was just no way in hell that I was going to be able to do this.

I was already uncomfortable and out of practice, but this was just way too much.

And he wanted to do it all?

Oral and all?

Oh, hell no!

My mouth was going to surely fall off!

Considering that I had been with Keymar pretty much my whole life, I wasn't exactly sure if I was the best sexually.

I was sure that I was decent and Keymar always seemed to be satisfied, but I wasn't so sure if another man would feel the same way.

And during my only other sexual encounter I hadn't done a thing except lay on my back, so I was sure that I needed a lot of work and improvement in that department.

This man was probably going to be bored to death!

Good…maybe he would never order me again.

"Envy he makes a lot of this happen. He knows a lot of important people, with a lot of connections. I tried to push him in the direction of one of our more *experienced* maids, one of his regulars, but he wants you. He specifically said: I want a piece of those curves. And come on because I'm sure that he's ready for you," Carmen said, standing to her feet.

I can't do this.

I don't want to do this.

I thought about how much of the money from the sign-on bonus I'd spent.

I'd paid every bill that I could so I knew that I didn't have the whole thing to give back to her if I changed my mind and broke the contract.

Not to mention, all of the other goodies that I had taken home and hidden in my closet over the last few days.

I guess I'd only imagined that it would be young, rich, and attractive men that would be into something like this.

Never did I consider that someone as old as dirt would be up here trying to get his freak on.

And he wanted *me* to suck *it*?

Yes, he was about to be disappointed.

But this was just my luck.

I had no business doing something like this in the first place.

Carmen got me dressed, sprayed a particular fragrance all over my body, handed me a whip, handcuffs and a bottle of expensive champagne.

Her face didn't appear to feel the least bit sorry for me but as she pulled my hair to the top of my head, her touch told me that maybe she felt just a little bit bad for me.

I could tell that she was concerned.

But whether it was concern for me or for the client, I wasn't exactly sure.

Regretfully, I followed her down the hall and soon she stopped in front of *my* room.

She looked at me.

Her face was so hard to read.

But I was sure that my face said exactly what was on my mind and in my heart.

I was disgusted.

"I left my key in my purse," I mumbled.

Carmen looked at me, and placed her key in the slot and then turned the knob.

I was sweating bullets but I entered the room and with no hesitation, Carmen closed the door behind me.

The next thing that I saw was enough to spoil a person's appetite for the next five years.

What in the hell...

To date, that had to be the longest three hours of my entire life!

The things that the old man had done to me were unheard of and the things that he wanted me to do to him were unspeakable.

I'd had to swallow my own vomit a couple of times just to try and get through it all.

I was so disgusted with myself that for the past hour or so, I'd been soaking in one of the soaker tubs, damn near trying to scrub my skin off.

I'd swallowed a whole bottle of mouth wash, and I was on my second bar of soap but no matter how many times I washed or gargled, I still felt filthy.

How could any woman, in her right mind, do something so degrading?

I'd never felt so used or worthless in all of my life.

Never did I imagine that I would be so desperate for money that I would become a very expensive, prostitute-maid.

This was not how my life was supposed to be.

I was supposed to be happily married with at least two kids by now; not somewhere selling my body on the top floor of a hotel just to get on my feet financially.

But there was no point in crying about it because for the next year, this was my reality.

After silently shedding a few tears, I realized that this is the decision that I'd made and it was time that I faced the facts and learned how to deal with it.

The hardest time was the first time, and it was over.

I'd made it through it.

It had shamed me but it hadn't killed me.

After another few minutes, I got myself together and changed into my regular maid outfit.

As soon as I was dressed, Carmen called my name.

She stared at me.

"Here. Take this tonight," she said and handed me a pill.

"It will help you sleep."

I didn't say a word, I only shook my head.

Carmen then handed me another envelope.

"$3100, that's your cut. I'm sure he tipped you pretty good too. You made it through and you made a good bit of money too. Go on home. Get yourself together. I'll see you tomorrow," she said.

I nodded my head, put the pill and the money in my purse and headed home.

As I walked, I thought about the maids that were ordered two and three times a day.

How on earth did they do it?

Why didn't it bother them to be used time and time again?

I overheard one maid telling another that she'd taken as much as $10,000 home in one day.

I could only imagine what she'd had to do for that type of money and just the thought of it started to make my stomach turn.

The things people do for money.

It started to thunder and I could smell the rain coming so I picked up the pace.

It was time for me to look into getting my car fixed or maybe even getting a new one.

Considering what Carmen had just given me, I had more than enough money for some kind of down payment.

Walking up to the house, I saw that the house that Rodney and his wife once shared was now up for sale.

I was hoping that whoever bought the house this time would at least be normal.

I didn't need another set of psycho, perverted neighbors.

I had enough problems on my plate already.

Checking for the mail, I took a deep breath and headed into the house with a smile on my face.

I left my hotel troubles outside of my front door just as I'd said that I would.

"How are you feeling?" I asked Tia later on that evening.

"I'm okay. I got my schedule worked out today. I only have classes three days a week and I got them as late as possible so that I could work with your schedule. You may have to see if you can go in a few hours earlier so that it all works out," she said to me.

"No, whatever it is will be fine. With my raise at work, I'm going to put Horizon in daycare. You may just have to get her there some mornings, or help pick her up some evenings. Or maybe she can just go part-time, on the days that you have school. That would save money," I said to her as if money was still an issue.

I was sure that I would be able to afford daycare, finally, but I didn't want to raise any red flags.

"Only if you have the money," Tia said.

She was so sweet, but just like anyone, she had another side to her.

But after replaying the way she'd spoken to Rodney and his wife that day, and the way that she'd handled the gun, I was sure that she was just as bad as I was if she was pushed to a certain point.

I couldn't help but wonder just how mean she could actually be. Maybe she was just as good as I was at keeping things hidden.

I had always been different; and not in a good way.

My mind was always somewhere that it wasn't supposed to be and I'd always had a side to me that was cold hearted and cruel.

It wasn't that I wanted to be.

Sometimes it just seemed as though it was out of my control.

Anyone who knew me knew that I am extremely overprotective and I love my family and my sisters with everything in me.

I would do anything for them.

I would lie for them, cheat for them…and even kill for them.

My sister, Josephine, who was only a year and a half younger than me, had been my best friend growing up.

As we got older, of course we went in separate directions, but we still had a bond that was unbreakable.

Before she'd gotten married to her current husband, she'd been madly in love with a guy named Roger.

But the catch to it was that Roger was madly in love with someone else.

I'd spotted him on several occasions being inappropriate with the same woman and when I approached him, he simply denied that anything was going on.

He walked around, pretending to love my sister and no matter how many questionable things he'd done, Josephine just couldn't seem to see him for who he really was.

So, I asked him nicely to leave her alone and let her be but he simply told me to mind my business.

Little did he know that she *was* my business!

So, one night as he walked to his car, he was hit and killed by what the police called a stray bullet.

But only I and Keymar's younger brother knew that it wasn't exactly a *stray*.

And he was now doing thirty years for drug charges, so it wasn't like anyone was ever going to find out our little secret.

As I said, I would do whatever I had to do to protect the people that I loved; even if it hurt them or someone else in the process.

Tia and I talked for a while longer and then we went our separate ways.

The rest of the day went by with a breeze and before I knew it, it was time to lie down and prepare for it all to start all over again the next day.

With Horizon already asleep, I kissed her forehead and then headed to my bedroom.

I locked the door behind me and then retrieved the envelopes from my purse.

I hadn't bothered to look in the one that I had received as a tip from the old client.

He'd just thrown it on the bed as I started to clean the room after he was finished with me.

I opened it and found that it was another thousand dollars.

Strangely, I smiled.

In less than a week, I had touched more money than I'd seen in forever.

Hurriedly, I took half of it and put it in my secret stash along with some of the left-over sign-on bonus money.

No matter what happened or how much money I made, I was positive that the hotel or Room 313 wouldn't get a day over a year from me.

I hid the box of cash back in the closet and then pulled out the pill from my purse.

I swallowed it without any water and then headed to shower even though I probably didn't need one.

Briefly, I thought about my failed attempt to give the old guy oral sex.

I must have been doing a horrible job because after only a minute or so, he'd asked me to stop.

I was so happy that I could have screamed but instead I was told to lie on my back so that he could *do* me.

Right on time, the shower water started to get cold and my thoughts of the ordeal abruptly came to a pause.

Thank goodness.

I needed to forget the memories…not relive them.

Stepping out of the shower and heading back into the bedroom, I didn't even bother to dry off.

I was feeling sluggish so I simply laid on the bed soaking wet.

I guess I should have at least asked her what kind of pill it was before accepting it, but I could only hope that it was something to help ease my mind and take away the awful thoughts of what had taken place in that hotel room that day.

My bedroom started to spin and my mind started racing.

And then suddenly… everything went pitch black.

The next morning, I woke up with a major headache. No matter what I tried, I just couldn't shake it.

There was no way that I was going to be able to go into the hotel.

I called Carmen to tell her that I wasn't feeling well.

I was surprised at how understanding she was, and with only a few questions, she told me to take the day off.

Good, I really needed to get my mind together.

"You're off today?"

"I wasn't. But I needed a day."

"Why? You just went back," Tia asked and grabbed a spoon and a tub of ice cream.

It was nine o'clock in the morning, but I didn't say a word since she was pregnant and all.

"Well, I need to look into some daycares and go look for another car," I said to her

"How? You haven't gotten paid yet."

"Oh, I thought I told you. I got a sign-on bonus."

"They give maids sign-on bonuses?"

"Head maids and office managers yes; because it's a salaried position."

"Oh," Tia shrugged and walked away.

That was pretty easy.

Next, I grabbed a phone book and called around to a few junk yards.

Within the next hour or so, I was being paid a few bucks and my old, useless car was being towed away.

There was no point in trying to trade in a car that was already broken and over fifteen years old.

Afterwards, we all got dressed and headed to the bus stop to begin our journey.

Hopefully this would be the last time riding the bus for a while and maybe even forever.

Maybe it was a bit tacky to arrive at a car lot by bus, but as long as I left with a car, I guess how I got there really didn't matter.

As we sat on the crowded bus, I glanced at the woman who sat across from us.

I couldn't believe how calm she was being as her daughter screamed at the top of her lungs.

Her daughter was out of control.

She was constantly asking her to stay still, and to be quiet but the small girl ignored her requests.

The other passengers frowned and whispered in disbelief at the mother's lack of authority.

If Horizon ever acted out like that in public she was going to see a very bad day.

Though I tried to look in the other direction, I couldn't help but stare at the child.

And then I would look back at the mother.

The longer I stared, the more and more I noticed a few things that were causing me to become unsettled.

For only a second I took my eyes off of the child and put them on my own.

I stared at my daughter Horizon and studied every curve and feature of her face.

She was her daddy's twin and she reminded me so much of him.

She had his eyes and his nose. She even had the same shade of skin.

The funny thing was that her father wasn't the only one that she looked a hell of a lot like.

I looked back at the misbehaving little girl and then up at her mother, who was surprisingly now staring at me.

She looked at me as though she found the look on my face amusing.

"Yep, she's Keymar's daughter," she said.

Huh?

Keymar who?

I know damn well that she wasn't talking about *my* Keymar.

We had been together since we were kids and he'd always been faithful to me.

I was sure of it.

"I know exactly who you are. I've seen you a few times before. My daughter, Keymarie is five. My name is Marie, so Keymarie was the perfect name for her. Keymar worked with my best friend's husband which is how we crossed each other's paths; at one of their events. We fooled around for almost a year and no one bothered to tell me that he was with you until I popped up pregnant. It wasn't until then that he'd told me that he had a fiancé and then he'd said that he didn't want anything to do with me or his daughter. He wouldn't see me. He stopped taking my calls. I remember coming by your house one evening. My best friend and I were going to expose him for the lying, cheating bastard that he was. But then I saw you two. You were playing outside with each other. You were laughing as he tickled you and he smiled and looked at you in a way that he'd never looked at me. And I guess I had a change of heart. We kept on driving and I decided that I was just going to raise my baby all on my own. It wasn't until things got hard and I lost my job that I thought to reach out to him again but found out that only a few days before…he'd died. We even came to the funeral. You were too busy crying and holding your new baby to notice that Keymarie and I had lingered at his casket just a little too long. So, yes, she is his daughter. And she is your daughter's sister. It's crazy. They almost look like twins," she said and stood up, grabbed her daughters hand and got off of the bus at the current stop.

Everyone, including my sister and daughter, sat staring at me.

As if they were waiting for my response or a reaction but I couldn't move.

Damn, she could have at least tried to reveal the proof in private instead of telling a bus full of people a truth that I didn't even know existed.

But more than being embarrassed, I was hurt.

I didn't know that it was possible for a dead man to break your heart, but my heart had been broken into a thousand tiny pieces.

I was always faithful to him.

And call me stupid, but I thought that he had always been faithful to me.

We'd had a bond so strong and it was so rare that loving or being with anybody else just didn't make sense.

He was the only person that I'd ever trusted completely. But to find out that not only had he been unfaithful to me, he'd conceived a child with another woman and then denied the child the right to know her father was just sickening to my soul.

I was so disappointed in him.

I was so furious that I didn't even try to stop the tears from falling from my eyes.

I'd given him my all, even after he was gone.

I'd loved him so much that I couldn't give another man my love or barely anything else out of loyalty to him.

But this was the thanks that I get?

To have some strange woman, on a bus, with a daughter that could have been my daughter's twin, tell me that my loyalty had been in vain.

It made me feel so stupid and ashamed to have ever even loved him.

He was lucky that he was already dead because if he wasn't I would have surely killed him.

But since he was already dead, the loyal, dedicated Envy had just died with him.

No more remaining by myself or running from love out of fear of losing the love that I had for him.

No more lonely nights because my mind, my heart and my loyalty still belonged to the only man I'd ever loved.

No more.

No, I was mad as hell and as of this day forward, Keymar and all of my feelings for him were history.

And to prove it, I was going to slang this pussy in every direction that I could!

Okay, so no, I probably wouldn't.

Especially since it was already a part of my current job description, but I was hurt and the only way to get revenge on a dead man was to stop holding on to him and truly let him go.

And as of right now, that was exactly what I was going to do.

We finally arrived at our stop and still speechless, I grabbed my purse, and Tia grabbed Horizon and we made our exit.

"Are you okay?" Tia asked once we were alone on the sidewalk.

I forced myself to grin at her.

"I will be. Now, let's go get us a new car," I said and headed in the direction of the car dealership.

For some reason, the hotel briefly crossed my mind.

Maybe now I could make this money and not feel so damn guilty about it.

Maybe.

***

I pulled in at the hotel in my new Toyota Camry.

Well, it wasn't all that new, but it was new to me.

I didn't know what to do with myself now that I didn't have to walk or ride the bus anymore and despite the way that I had to earn the money, I couldn't help but be thankful for it.

I walked into the hotel in my regular maid outfit and headed towards Carmen's office.

She was sitting at the desk, with her eyes closed.

She opened them at the sound of my footsteps.

"Feeling better?" she said.

I simply nodded.

"Did you get the car?" she asked.

I nodded again.

The dealership had to verify my employment with Carmen.

I'd sent her a text regarding what I needed her to say.

I wasn't sure if she was going to do it, but she had. She'd lied on my behalf and said that I was the head maid, on salary, and that I had been there for over two years.

"Thank you."

"No thanks needed," she said and got up and headed to the wall.

She was still all over me, more so than she was with the other girls.

I guessed it was because I was still new.

The thirteenth floor was quiet.

Either the other maids hadn't started rolling in yet, were already gone home, or they were already busy.

Some of the maids worked at night.

I only worked day hours because of Horizon.

"I need you to get yourself together. You've been ordered already…twice," Carmen said.

She briefly talked numbers and told me that before any tips unless I was ordered again before it was time for me to leave, I would be taking home another three thousand dollars.

She'd said that I had been ordered for just basic sex, both times, and that this time should be easier for me.

It all still seemed so unreal.

But as I headed to my room, I knew that what was about to take place was absolutely…. real.

Here I was, about to give myself to another stranger, for money, and it just didn't get any more real than that.

"Oh, by the way, you should work on your oral sex. I've heard that you could use a little practice. Good oral means good tips," Carmen said behind me.

Luckily no one else was around or she would have embarrassed the hell out of me.

I stared at the 313 on the door in front of me.

Here we go again.

"Hi," the gentleman said.

I was hesitant to look in his direction but once I did, I was surprised by my reaction.

At the sight of the client, I *accidently* licked my lips.

The man that was standing in front of me was beautiful, if I was able to identify him as such.

He was tall, dark and deliciously handsome.

The broadness of his shoulders had me mesmerized.

He was wearing a high priced black suit with the cutest little white and black bow tie.

The Rolex on his arm beamed as bright as an evening star. He had the most beautiful white teeth and the most adorable smile that I'd ever seen.

He surely didn't look as though he belonged here and I just couldn't believe that he had to settle for paying for a piece of ass.

No, I would never believe that he couldn't have any woman that he wanted.

Hell, he could have me…for free.

I just wanted to take him home so that I could look at him all day.

"What's your name?"

I looked at him confused at first, but then I remembered that Carmen said that they never revealed our names; we were labeled with a number.

I figured that I should probably make up a name, but after all, who would believe that my real name was Envy?

"Envy," I said and stood still.

I watched him look me up and down.

He looked at my hips and at every single curve of my body with lust in his eye.

Uh, oh, he was hypnotized.

It was my turn to fully check him out.

I scanned him once again from top to bottom.

I couldn't help but become aroused.

I couldn't help but want him.

It had been so long since a man had turned me on or even caught my interest that the feeling not only surprised me, but it made me extremely anxious.

I guess it was because I was so used to being so guarded but since the bus incident yesterday, I had a whole new attitude and my heart was as cold as ice.

Men hurt women that love them all the time and they cheat on the ones that are faithful to them so it was time to use them the same way that they used us.

I had what he wanted and he had what I needed.

It was just that simple.

I still wasn't sure of all the code names yet, but Carmen had mentioned that he had ordered just the basics, but I didn't want to be basic.

Not with him.

I was going to allow myself to enjoy this---this time.

Yes, this one was for me.

I took a deep breath and walked closer to him.

I won't pretend as though I wasn't still nervous or uneasy because I was.

But I wasn't as grossed out and uncomfortable as I was before or as I should have been.

Not with him.

To be honest, he seemed a little nervous as if this was his first time at the *rodeo*.

But I was sure that it wasn't.

"Before we begin can I ask you for a favor?" I asked him.

He looked as though he didn't know how to answer the question or as if he didn't know if he was able to do "favors".

But I was sure that he wouldn't mind doing this one.

He nodded his head as I stood only inches away from him.

"Can you teach me how to give *good head*?" I asked him.

His eyes widen and it was as though he'd stopped breathing for only a second.

But soon after, his lips curled up into a small smile and he shrugged his shoulders and nodded his head.

When he unbuckled his belt, and dropped his pants, I knew that he was onboard.

Well…let's get this party started!

****
*

Chapter FOUR

After only two months, I'd made so much money that I'd lost count.

And the craziest thing of all was that I was starting to like it.

In a weird way, it had become…normal.

I'd even lost count of how many men I'd been with.

Here lately, Room 313 was where everyone wanted to be.

Most of the time I was ordered at least twice a day and I was something like the new hot thing on the floor.

I was being ordered so much and so often that I was being *reserved*; which meant that the men would pay extra to ensure that I was available and not busy at the time that they arrived at the hotel.

Carmen said that the demand for a woman had never been so extreme to the point that she made money just by *reserving my curves*. So, the way I saw it was that she now needed me, just as much as I'd once needed her.

I still kept my distance from the other women and so far, I hadn't made a single *friend*.

But I was fine with that.

As long as I had my sister, I didn't really need anyone else.

Speaking of my sister, Tia was dealing with her pregnancy pretty well.

She was going to classes as promised, helping with Horizon and still managing to keep her body together.

She hadn't gained but ten pounds, if that much, although she ate like a horse.

But she was my rock at the moment and part of my motivation.

She still didn't know the truth about what I did at the hotel and I had no plans on telling her either.

I made sure that she had everything that she needed and then some.

I gave her money every week for the days that she looked after Horizon.

Of course, she would refuse it but I would always leave it for her on her dresser the next morning before work and I wouldn't take it back.

She was about to have a baby.

I was sure that there were little things that she wanted to buy, so she needed money.

And I had plenty to give.

I dropped Tia off at the doctor's office and Horizon and I headed to grab some lunch.

I figured that Tia was going to be there for at least three hours, as always, so we had plenty of time to spare.

It was the end of October but it was still pretty warm so Horizon and I stopped for lunch at an outside café.

After ordering and getting Horizon settled, I stared at the couple sitting across from us.

They appeared to be a happy family.

There was a husband, a wife and a little boy and girl.

They talked and laughed as they ate and made jokes with each other.

I couldn't help but smile at them.

What I wouldn't give for that life; that completion.

Not just for my sake, but for my daughter's as well.

That was the life that we were supposed to have.

I was supposed to be married and raising her with the man of my dreams and the love of my life, but things hadn't turned out that way.

It's funny how things never turn out the way that you want them to but in the end, they usually end up being what they are supposed to be.

I forced myself to hold back the tears as the waitress placed our food on the table.

One day, is all that I could think to myself as I prepared Horizon to eat her lunch.

One day that will be me.

One day that would be us.

"Excuse me, but do I know you from somewhere?"

Immediately I became nervous at the tap on my shoulder.

I hesitated to turn around.

My biggest fear was to see one of the men from the hotel out in public.

It would remind me of my secret life, and I didn't want to be reminded of anything that I did on the thirteenth floor.

When I wasn't there I just wanted to enjoy being normal.

Just being me.

I turned around to look at the man whose hand was still on my shoulder.

Surprisingly, he wasn't one of the men from the hotel. In fact, I didn't know him at all.

I'd never seen him before.

"Um," I started to say but he interrupted me.

"I'm just kidding. I don't know you. I'm just a little out of practice when it comes to, well---I'm Silas."

I studied him as I shook his outstretch hand.

For the most part, he was fairly attractive.

Since I'd only been in a relationship with Keymar, I hadn't developed a certain type, but I was sure that whatever it was, he was it.

He was dressed casually.

A little inappropriate for the weather, but I could only assume that it was due to his profession.

He was wearing a long-sleeved button up shirt, with dress pants, suspenders and a black tie.

He had strong, bold facial features and his brown eyes stood out the most.

I'd say that he was a strong seven or maybe even an eight.

Judging by his accent, I was sure that he was of African descent; but his shade of skin was a warm, soft brown complexion.

His skin reminded me of soothing caramel, and the more I stared at him, the more my mouth began to water.

"I'm Envy," I cleared my voice.

"Envy? Interesting name. I guess I sounded pretty corny approaching you but I just couldn't leave without saying something. When I saw you take your seat, I knew that I would regret it if I didn't come over here and say something to you."

Okay, so I was flattered.

It had been a while since anyone had genuinely shown interest in me and not just because they'd purchased me.

I couldn't help but wonder what he meant by the statement that he was out of practice.

I figured that now wasn't the appropriate moment to ask him too many questions so I just smiled.

Was I really ready for something like this?

Looking back at the happy family, I got my answer.

Hell yeah!

***

I walked slowly towards the door.

I wasn't exactly sure what it was until I was close enough to see it.

Someone had placed a piece of paper that said "Whore" on my front door and a big butcher's knife was stabbed right in the center of it.

What the hell is going on here?

And more importantly, who knew about my secret?

I removed the knife and crumbled up the piece of paper.

I checked my surroundings just to see if I saw something or someone out of place, but everything looked normal.

Who would have done something like this?

I was sure that it had to be connected to my job at the hotel, but why would someone have come to my home and done this?

Furthermore, how did they find out where I lived?

I was definitely feeling some kind of way but I placed the items in my purse and entered the house as though nothing was wrong.

And the drama begins…

"Do I look okay?" I asked Tia.

I'd changed my outfit all of ten times.

I was going on my first date with Silas and I wanted to look perfect.

I hadn't been on a date in years and I was as nervous as a woman wearing a weave ponytail with only two Bobby pins in it.

Have you ever done that?

I'm telling you, it will have a sista' on edge all day!

"You look fine Envy. And those shoes…when did you get those? And are they Louis Vuitton?" Tia questioned me coming closer.

Though I had a ton of free items from the hotel, I kept most of it hidden.

I figured that I would have to ease out one item at a time as though I'd been saving up for it.

Still yet, I didn't think that Tia was going to believe that I'd bought these shoes with my own money…so I lied.

"Well, I was cleaning up a room one day and someone had left them behind. I held on to them for a while but when no one ever called or came back to claim them, I brought them home. They were my size, so I thought what the hell…I might as well keep them."

I studied Tia's face.

She believed me.

She looked at them once more and shrugged her shoulders.

"Well, I will be borrowing those once I drop this load," she said rubbing her stomach.

She continued to help me get dressed and it seemed like only seconds later, the doorbell chimed.

I kissed Horizon and smiled at Tia.

Here goes nothing.

"So, what is it that you do?" I asked Silas.

We hadn't talked on the phone but a few times and never for very long.

Usually when he called I was at the hotel and though I would promise to call him back once I was home, most of the time, I forgot.

"Well, the short answer is, I'm a doctor. I'm an Endocrinologist. Basically, I deal with people with diabetes."

A doctor?

Little ole' me snagged a doctor?

I wanted to toot my own horn, but now wasn't the time or the place.

"And you?" Silas asked.

I didn't know whether to tell him the truth or to lie. How could I tell him that I was a maid…and a prostitute?

But I had to say something.

"Well, I know it isn't much of a job, but I run a hotel."

At least that didn't sound as bad.

"Hey, there's nothing wrong with that."

"I've been there for years but I'm studying to become a medical assistant as well."

"See. Nothing is sexier than a woman with a plan," Silas smiled and touched my hand.

Instantly a chill slithered down my spine, around to my stomach, skipped over my thighs, and *tickled my fancy*.

For some reason, I had become extremely horny.

Though I hadn't been in a serious relationship in a while, Tia told me what was newly expected of women on dates these days.

Basically, she said if I was just looking to be pleased, I should go home with him at the end of the date.

But if I was truly interested, he couldn't be introduced to *the lady* that lived in between my thighs until at least date number three or four.

She'd said that since sex was so easy to get these days, it was even tougher to get a real commitment.

So, I guess that meant that I had to keep my goodies to myself.

At least for a little while.

"So, you mentioned that you were out of practice that day. What did you mean?"

Silas took a sip of his champagne and then gazed into my eyes.

His eyes were filled with so much sincerity that it made me feel so safe and secure.

He made me feel…comfortable.

"I used to be married."

Past tense.

"My wife and my daughter died in a car accident about a year ago. They were hit head on by a drunk driver. They both died at the scene. I'd been married for a little over ten years," Silas said.

"I'm so sorry," I said touching his hand.

He smiled at me.

"It's okay. So, I guess getting back into the dating game hasn't been easy for me. What about you? Have you ever been married?"

"No. I was engaged to my daughter's father. But he died as well. He went to sleep one night and just didn't wake back up. We'd been together since we were kids. He was the only man I've ever been with"

Hell, I had been telling the same story for so long that there wasn't any point in changing it up now.

He didn't need to know that I'd gone from two men to a few from twenty in just a few months.

And I still had months and months to go.

The rest of the dinner, we talked and laughed and it felt so good to be in his company.

I could get use to this.

This was what life and love was all about.

"How about we drive around for a while and just talk," Silas suggested.

"I would really like that," I smiled.

Just as we pulled off, my cell phone began to ring.

It was Carmen.

Hesitantly, I answered.

"Hello."

"Envy, I need you to come in. Mr., *you know who*, had a delayed flight and of course, he only wants you."

I knew exactly who she was talking about...Gerald.

He was the same man that had turned me into a *pro* in the sheets, especially the oral sex department and he was the only man that I actually enjoyed sleeping with at the hotel.

Since that day, I was now the only one that he ordered.

Gerald was some type of oil tycoon who had more money than he knew what to do with it.

The problem was that he felt as though he'd worked too hard to have to share it with anyone long term so he refused to settle down and get married.

He said that no one deserved to share his millions or potentially take half of them if things took a turn for the worst.

I guess I could understand his reasoning but at the end of the day, love was all that really mattered.

What was the point in having money if you had to spend it all alone?

"If you come tonight for a few hours, you can have the day off tomorrow," Carmen bribed me and it worked.

I hung up the phone and explained to Silas that I had an emergency at work.

He understood, drove me home and after we shared our first kiss, I was in my car, heading for the hotel.

I walked in the hotel, still in my date attire.

Carmen was waiting for me in her downstairs office and as soon as I entered, up the elevator we went.

I no longer needed her coaching.

I knew exactly what to do and once I was freshened up, I headed to my room where Gerald was waiting for me.

"So, someone is being picky tonight huh?"

Gerald smiled at the sight of me.

Really, he had become sort of a friend.

Sure, he got what he paid for, but we would also just spend hours talking about everything under the sun.

It was as though he felt that he could be completely honest with me.

He walked over to me and hugged me.

He often did that, which I had gotten used to.

It was almost as if for those few hours, I was his woman.

"Sit down," he said.

I did as he instructed, thinking that he wanted to try something new.

"Envy, I want you to quit. Quit and run away with me," he said.

I looked at him confused.

"I know that this isn't the idea way of meeting and getting to know someone, but no one knows me better than you. It's like I can be honest with you. I'm sure that there's other things that I need to know, and that's okay, just quit and run away with me," Gerald said.

Is he serious?

I believe that he is.

"Gerald, you know I'm under contract and—"

"I'll buy it out."

He really was serious.

My mind was trying to sort everything out.

Buying me out of the contract sounded amazing.

But did we know each other well enough to just run off and be together?

All we had between us was sex and conversation.

Despite my current situation, I wanted more than that.

I still wanted, and needed love.

"Gerald, I have a daughter."

"So, she can come too," he said.

Okay, so maybe I should take him up on his offer.

Wait a minute…Tia.

I still had to look out for Tia.

She was pregnant and still in college and she needed me to be there for her.

I was all that she had.

"I'm sorry, but Gerald, I just can't."

He looked at me disappointedly and shook his head.

"This will be my last time coming here and my last time seeing you. I met someone. I guess I will probably marry her and settle down. All of your talks and advice finally got to me and I guess I thought that maybe you and I…"

I placed my finger on his lips.

I did feel some kind of way that I would never see him again.

As weird as it may sound, we did have some kind of bond or attachment to each other.

What I wouldn't give to be able to drop everything and become a millionaire's wife, but I had other priorities that I just couldn't leave behind.

Maybe Tia could come along and put her education on hold and start again wherever we settled.

Maybe.

And then again…maybe not.

I leaned in and kissed Gerald.

We kissed all the time, though it wasn't required, but this time, I kissed him with everything that I had in me.

And he was obviously kissing me with everything that he had in him as well.

Our kiss was full of sorrow, regret and maybe even just a little bit of hope, but I knew that this was the end of our road.

Gerald laid me on my back and started to caress my hips and my thighs.

His eyes were closed as he continued to rub every curve of my body.

It was as though he was trying to lock my touch into his memory.

The dress came up and the panties soon came down.

No words were spoken, and it seemed as though we were both struggling to catch our breaths.

The room felt extremely small and there was so much passion between us that it was almost unbearable.

Gerald entered me, and moaned softly, regretfully, as if he couldn't believe that this was going to be the last time that he touched me.

It was prohibited to have sex without protection, but this wasn't the first time for us.

I didn't have to worry about getting pregnant because I'd gotten the birth control that lasted five years after having Horizon. And even if I hadn't, Carmen kept a stash of *the morning after* pills.

As I said, the thirteenth floor didn't play around.

In some sick and twisted way, we had developed some type of connection, but whatever it was that we shared wasn't love and I would be crazy to think otherwise.

I enjoyed the pleasures of him one final time and once it was all said and done Gerald stood looking at me by the room door.

I smiled at him but he didn't smile back.

He just looked at me.

I was almost stupid enough to actually think that he might even really care for me but, how could he?

No matter what he said, he would never respect a woman like me.

Seeing him place the wad of money as a tip on the table by the door only confirmed that no matter what he said, he saw me for what I was.

An *executive* maid, that took care of *executive* guests.

Translation…a very over-priced whore.

No more…no less.

"Goodbye Envy," he said and without waiting for me to respond, he turned his back to me and exited the room.

I took a second to think and then I stood to my feet and prepared to change the sheets.

If only we'd met under different circumstances but unfortunately, for me, we hadn't.

***

"Get on your knees so that I can piss on you," the middle-aged white man said to me.

I looked at him as though he'd spoken in some kind of foreign language.

I'd heard that some of the men wanted weird and crazy things done, but I had yet to encounter it; until now.

"Did you hear what I said? Get on your knees…now," he said again.

I wanted to curse him out from here to Mexico but I knew that I couldn't.

I knew that I was going to have to do exactly what he'd said. As I got on my knees, I'd never felt so low in all of my life.

Since I'd been making so much money, I'd forgotten that what I was doing was a disgrace, but the warmth of the piss on my back, reminded me of what and who I had become.

The man continued to pee on me, and laughed the entire time.

I'll admit, I wanted to cry my eyes out but what was the point in crying?

This is the type of humiliation that I'd signed up for so I had to put on my big girl panties and deal with it.

But it wasn't easy.

Leaving the hotel, I was angry.

I was angry at everything that had happened to me.

I was angry at what I'd become.

I was angry because I hadn't had a choice.

And I was angry because I knew that no matter what, I couldn't change it for a little while longer.

My phone started to ring and at the sight of Silas's face I frowned.

He had been nothing but good to me so far but I couldn't help but wonder if he would still want me if he knew the truth about me.

My guess was that he wouldn't.

He would be a fool to want a whore like me.

Feeling down and out, I arrived at home to find Tia and Horizon on the front porch.

They appeared to be having some kind of conversation and when they noticed me, they both smiled.

I took a deep breath and tried my best to shake off my frustrations.

I couldn't let them see how down and disturbed I was.

And I knew that though Tia might not say much, she was definitely paying attention.

"How was your day?" she asked rubbing her belly.

"It was okay. Did I get any mail?" I asked her as I hugged Horizon.

Tia looked at me.

I could tell that she had something to say.

"Um, yes, but you got something kind of strange," she said and stood up to head into the house.

Horizon and I followed her to the kitchen.

"This was just sitting in the mail box. Since it didn't have a name on it, I opened it. It's rings," Tia looked at me confused.

I looked in the envelope to find that it was indeed a set of rings.

The brides set as well as the groom's.

Okay, so first I found the strange *whore* note stabbed to the front door, and now someone had placed their rings in my mailbox?

Something just wasn't adding up.

Though I tried to avoid all married men at the hotel, as Carmen said, sometimes, we just never know.

But this was the actions of somebody's wife.

And I was going to figure out whose.

****

*****

Chapter FIVE

"Merry Christmas!" I squealed.

I couldn't believe that I'd gotten up before Horizon but it'd given me a chance to pull out the rest of her goodies from the closet.

At the sound of my voice, she lifted her head, smiled, and then Horizon ran to the Christmas tree and started in on her gifts.

After about five minutes, Tia appeared in the living room.

She was as big as a house!

She was having a little boy and I couldn't wait for his arrival!

I figured by the time that he was born, I would only have a few more months at the hotel and then I was going to stay home and spoil him like crazy while his mama prepared to join the working world and put that hard-earned degree that she would have to good use.

I'd saved a ton of money, and I knew that we were going to be okay for quite some time after I left the hotel. But considering that I was almost half way through my medical assistant program I knew that eventually after leaving the hotel, I would look for a job in that field.

I was sure that finding a job wouldn't be as challenging as it had been before and from the looks of it, everything was going to be just fine.

"Go open your stuff," I said to Tia.

She just looked at me.

Then she turned around and disappeared for a few minutes.

"Well, I got you a little something too," she said and reached me a small box.

"You shouldn't have. The money that I give you is for you and the baby," I said to her, taking the box from her hands.

I opened it and immediately I smiled at the sight of the charm bracelet.

It was silver and possessed charms of pretty much everything that I liked to do or things that she'd known that I was good at.

She'd even put a charm of a maid on it.

"Aw, thank you. You didn't have to buy me anything," I said standing up to hug her.

She struggled to embrace me over her belly and then she headed to the tree.

"So, which one?" she asked.

I pointed to all twenty presents on the right side of the tree.

"All of these?"

I smiled at her.

"All of those. Of course, you and the baby count as one you know," I said as she noticed that I'd purchased a brand-new crib for the baby.

I was hoping that she wouldn't question me too much about the money but if she did I was simply going to say that I received another bonus check for the holidays.

But luckily, despite that fact that I'd purchased her some pretty expensive gifts she didn't ask me any questions.

Not even one.

The chiming of the doorbell stole my attention and I headed towards the door.

"Merry Christmas baby," Silas smiled.

I guess you could say that we were dating.

And everything was going just fine.

Silas got plenty of my free time and I had to admit that I was really enjoying his company.

He was funny, smart and the perfect gentleman.

I loved that he treated me like a queen and I liked that he complimented me and spoiled me, regularly.

Being with him was even better than it had been with Keymar.

And I never thought that I would say those words.

Silas and I had yet to cross the *sex-line* and to be honest I hadn't been in that big of a rush.

I gave away enough ass on the regular because I had to so, I'd wanted to take my time with giving it up for pleasure.

Oh, but it was coming.

He handed me a bag full of goodies and I kissed him on the cheek.

"Really? It's Christmas," Silas smiled and kissed my lips.

"Eww! Y'all nasty," Tia whined and her and Horizon continued going through their gifts.

"I have a gift for you too, but you can't get it until later," I smiled but not as big as Silas did.

He'd been more than patient with me but I was sure that he was *overdue*.

He was still a man.

And it was time for me to take care of his needs.

I was just a tad bit nervous as to what would come after we had sex.

Would it officially mean that we were a couple?

Would things between us change?

I couldn't help but wonder if it was in my best interest to still keep some kind of emotional and even a little physical distance from him; at least until I was done with the hotel.

I didn't want to risk him finding out the truth and then walking away; especially since I was already almost in love with him.

No, I hadn't had the most experience with being in love more than once, but if my memory served me correctly, it surely felt a hell of a lot like this.

Maybe it was too soon to feel this way, so I tried my best to keep my emotions in check.

But I was definitely starting to feel something for him.

And I could only hope that he was starting to feel something for me too.

The rest of the day went by smoothly and before I knew it, the day was gone and seeing that Tia and Horizon were fast asleep on the living room floor, it was time for Silas and I to get nasty!

I left him for a few moments and headed to my bed room to shower and prepare myself for my performance.

I'd chosen to dress up like Mrs. Clause---a topless, sexier version of course.

I only wore the bottom half of the outfit, a red lace bra and thong combo, a hat, the sexiest little Mrs. Clause glasses, fish net stockings and an expensive pair of pumps that I'd gotten from the hotel.

I lit candles, turned on soft music and made sure that everything was in its proper place.

Working on the thirteenth floor I'd learned a few things whether it was from the clients or from eavesdropping on conversations that the other women seldom had.

"Silas?" I called out to him.

I heard him coming down the hallway.

"I'm in here"

He'd never been back to my bedroom before and he smiled at the sight of it.

Let's just say that though I didn't make my room at the hotel as comfortable as I could've my bedroom at home was everything that a room was supposed to be.

It was one of the only rooms in the house that you could actually tell that I was making good money.

I'd upgraded to a two-thousand-dollar king sized bedroom suite; pillow-top mattresses, silk sheets, huge paintings, a sixty-inch TV on the wall and a five-hundred-dollar rug.

My bedroom was my own little paradise and I couldn't wait to get home to it after a long day at the hotel.

Silas smiled at my partial outfit and leaned in to kiss me but I moved away.

"Sorry, but I'm running this show," I said.

I led him to the bathroom and left him there to shower.

When he appeared back in the bedroom, my juices instantly soaked the lining of the red thong that I was wearing.

I eyed him hungrily.

His skin was so smooth and creamy and I just couldn't wait to taste him.

Of course, he was a doctor, one that dealt with diabetes, so he was in tip top shape.

He had abs and everything.

Not to mention that I just loved to listen to him talk.

I was surprised that I had held out for as long as I had.

But now it was time to get down to business!

Since I'd been at the hotel, my sex-game had gone from a one to a ten.

I was a bad, bad girl in the *sack*, and I wasn't afraid to show it...at least not anymore.

I could cause a penis to *spit-up* in just three minutes' flat, not to mention the tricks that I'd learned whether I was on top, bottom, and even from behind.

Never did I ever think that I would become so comfortable sexually, but now that I was, I knew that what I had in between my legs was dangerous.

Hopefully Silas could handle it.

He walked closer to me and I didn't hesitate to place *him* in my mouth.

It took only a second or two for his manhood to start to swell and I waited patiently for it to reach its full *potential*.

My tongue obeyed the silent orders of my mind as it swiftly licked his *wood* from the tip of the *head*, down the shaft and even briefly bathed his balls.

Silas moaned softly as I grabbed his hands and placed them on my head.

I'd become accustomed to getting my hair pulled while I *serviced* a man with my mouth, and I actually liked it.

Silas quickly caught on, grabbed my hair and I got to work.

My hands moved speedily as my mouth and throat sucked and swallowed until Silas's knees started to buckle.

Suddenly he became stiff and I knew that his *missile* was about ready to *fire* but just before he could fill my mouth with his juices, I pulled my head away.

If looks could kill…I would have been a dead woman.

But I had my reasons.

I stood up, motioned for him to lie on the bed as I headed to shut my bedroom door.

Slowly I walked towards him, taking off everything that I had on piece by piece.

I could tell that Silas was growing impatient and it looked as though he wanted to curse me out for taking my time, but he said nothing.

I smiled at him as I crawled onto the bed.

I turned backwards and smiled as he moaned while he entered me.

I made myself comfortable and started to rock my hips.

Once Silas joined in, I knew that this was about to be some of the best sex of my life.

Showtime.

The next morning, after cuddling and chatting for an hour or so, we decided to take my sister and my daughter out for breakfast.

Once everyone was dressed, we headed out the door but soon found that we weren't going anywhere, anytime soon.

Both my car and Silas's sat in my driveway with four flat tires, each, and busted windshields.

Immediately, instinctively, I started rehearsing in my head my explanation to Silas.

But that would come later.

As for now, I was pissed what you would call, the Hell off!

I was sure that whoever had done this was the same person that had stabbed the piece of paper on my front door and the same person that had left the wedding rings in the mailbox.

I still didn't know who it was behind it all but it was starting to get on my last damn nerve!

Messing with my personal property was just going too damn far!

Well, I guess if it was someone's angry wife, her husband's *dick* was her personal property; but she needed to take that up with him.

I never willingly slept with a married man.

If he was married, I didn't know it and so in my opinion, I couldn't be held accountable.

It wasn't my fault---it was his.

And as crazy as it all sounded, I really felt that way.

But some way, somehow, if it was connected to one of the men at the hotel, then that would mean that somehow the wife had to find out who I was.

I'd told a few of them that my name was Envy.

Maybe they'd accidently said my name or something.

Maybe a wife had followed her husband to the hotel.

But how did they know that it was me?

And to start harassing me, coming by house, and doing unnecessary stuff was going just a little overboard and it was surely going to get *her* ass kicked…whoever she was.

To be honest, this was some crazy stuff that I would probably do under the same circumstances.

But I would at least ask a few questions first.

Damn!

Tia took Horizon back into the house and Silas looked at me.

I was thinking of something that might sound valid or at least half way believable.

It had to be believable.

"Envy, what's going on here?"

I took a deep breath.

"Well, the mother of my deceased fiancé's other child and I don't get along. She's always coming by here, doing stupid stuff out of the blue because she's mad that he left me everything. I'll admit, yes, I've done things to her in the past and we've had it out on several occasions but I'm just trying to move on with my life. I'm assuming she got offended because I told her that I didn't want the girls to see each other for Christmas. I know that's her sister and all but I still have a hard time accepting it. After all, he cheated on me with her. I'm sure she did this. Or put someone up to it," I said exhaling.

Where in the hell did I pull that lie from?

I didn't know that I had one like that in me but from the look on Silas's face, it was working.

I probably could have come up with something less farfetched but obviously for him it was just right.

I would do and say anything to keep Silas from finding out the truth.

Silas didn't say much except that it was time for me to take legal action against her.

After his comment, he embraced me and then got on the phone to see what he could do about our vehicles.

Whoa, that was a close one!

I was in the clear with Silas, but no matter what Silas believed, the truth was the bigger problem.

I didn't like the idea of someone coming to my home and messing with my stuff.

I didn't like knowing that whoever the person was periodically showed up at the place where my daughter laid her head.

Obviously, they had a few screws loose so it was time to do some investigation.

One of the men that I was sleeping with at the hotel was married and I was going to find out which one it was.

***

Silas and I hadn't spent much time together since the day after Christmas.

As far as I knew, he wasn't mad or anything.

Work just had been busy for us both lately.

But it was my day off from the hotel so I decided that I was going to surprise him at work with lunch.

I'd never gone to his job before though he'd told me the name of it on several occasions.

I figured that I had to do something a little special for him just to make sure that things were still okay between us.

After parking my car and checking my reflection in the driver's side window, I headed towards the building.

The office was nice and cozy and a little quiet for a doctor's office.

"Hello, I'm here to see Dr. Silas Okeke," I said politely.

The receptionist smiled at me.

"Who?"

"Um…Dr. Silas Okeke," I repeated.

"Are you sure that he works at this facility? We don't have a doctor on staff by that name."

I frowned at her comment and apologized for wasting her time.

Heading back to my car, I couldn't seem to get my thoughts together.

Why would he lie about where he worked?

And then it hit me…maybe he was just like me.

Did he have a job that he wasn't exactly proud of?

From the looks of his house, car, and the fact that he always paid for everything when we went out, he definitely had a good bit of income coming in from somewhere.

But if it wasn't from being a doctor…then what was it from?

What is it that he did for a living and why was he ashamed of it?

It couldn't be as bad as what I did.

I went back and forth, mentally, as to whether or not I wanted to mention my discovery to Silas or not.

To be honest, I was a tad bit afraid of what he might say.

Once I'd decided to keep my mouth shut for a while, I called Silas before pulling off.

"Hi beautiful, how are you today?" Silas asked.

"I'm doing fine. Are you at work?" I asked him.

"Of course."

Liar!

Or maybe he wasn't lying about being at work but he damn sure wasn't a doctor for the place that he'd told me.

But I played along.

"Oh, well, I was thinking that maybe I would stop by and bring you lunch."

"I was just heading out. I'll meet you," Silas said.

As I drove down the street, I threw the lunch that I was going to take him out the window.

I couldn't believe that he was lying about where he worked and what he did for a living.

If he was lying about that…what else was he lying about?

I didn't know if I had the right to be upset at the fact that he wasn't being truthful, but I was.

I knew my reasoning behind my lies, so I couldn't help but wonder what it was that he didn't want me to know.

What in the hell is he hiding?

Seeing him waiting for me outside of the restaurant, I decided that I wouldn't say a word but he had better believe that I was on to him.

I was going to find out what I needed and wanted to know about him.

Even if it killed me.

****

Chapter SIX

I sat in my car, watching Silas leave the parking lot of the hotel.

The funny thing was that I'd told him that I worked at a completely different hotel so I knew that his visit there had nothing to do with me.

So, the question was...what in the hell was he doing here?

Had I gone into the hotel when I'd first arrived we would have surely run into each other but instead I'd been sitting in my car for the last few minutes, listening to music and trying to get myself together.

And just as I'd turned off the radio, there he was, Silas, walking to his car, getting in, and hurriedly driving away.

Why was he there in the first place?

I found my phone to call him.

I already knew that he was going to lie, but I thought that I would ask him anyway, just to see what he was going to say.

"Hey, how's your day going?"

"Good. I'm tired already and I have an ass load of patients to see today. I was just taking a little break. I had to make a quick run but I'm headed back to my office now. What are you up to?"

Well, at least he didn't exactly lie about being out and about but he was still pretending to be a doctor.

I didn't tell him that I saw him at the hotel but little by little I was starting to get a bad feeling about him.

To be honest, I was feeling extremely disappointed because my heart was already attached to him.

The first night that we'd had sex had confirmed that I was falling in love with him.

The thought that things weren't going to be what I'd hoped they would be troubled my soul.

Silas was so loving, kind and he even had a crazy sense of humor.

He always made me laugh and smile and now I wasn't even sure who he really was.

And then a troubling thought crossed my mind.

What if he was a client of the thirteenth floor?

What if he was one of those executive guests that paid one of my fellow floozies for sex?

No, he wasn't that type of guy…was he?

I wasn't sure of where the money was coming from, but from the looks of it he had a good bit of it; which made him a *potential* client of ours.

We *serviced* plenty of doctors, regularly, though I was sure that Silas wasn't a doctor at all.

I got out of the car still thinking of Silas and his reasoning for being at the hotel.

I couldn't help but wonder what he would have said or what he would have done if he'd saw me there, especially if he'd seen me selling my body on the top floor.

And then again, what if he already knew?

The clients looked through a *menu* to pick the type of woman that they wanted.

Every woman on the floor had her own page which showed a picture of her body and her work days and hours.

If they were already ordered, or in my case, *reserved*, Carmen notified the client and from that point they would have to choose someone else.

So, what if Silas was a client and already knew who I really was?

How embarrassing would that be?

I didn't know what to think as I headed towards Carmen's office but I was sure of one thing and that was that it was probably in my best interest to go ahead and leave Silas alone.

But that was going to be easier said than done.

***

"How about we go get something to eat?" Carmen suggested.

Though I worked for her again, we didn't have the type of relationship that we had in the past.

Truth be told, I just didn't like the *real* her.

I never said a word to her unless it was about business or about one of the clients.

Our conversations were always short and straight to the point.

I wanted it to be clear that I was just her employee…not her friend.

I was strictly there for the money…at least at first I was.

Money was no longer the issue so now I was just there because I was under contract.

I was going to decline, especially since Silas was supposed to be coming over for dinner that evening, and I planned to try to have a much-needed conversation with him, but there were a few things that I wanted to talk to Carmen about as well so I informed Tia and Silas of my change of plans and Carmen and I headed out to eat.

Carmen was older, but she was gorgeous.

She had a rocking body too.

She walked, looked and even smelled like money.

And I do mean literally smelled like money.

Just by looking at her you could tell that she enjoyed the finer things in life and you would have to step to her correct if you had the balls to step to her at all.

I was sure that other regular employees had to question just how much money it was that Carmen made being what she portrayed to be for the hotel.

I was surprised that no one had ever questioned it.

Carmen and I entered a five-star restaurant and after a quick phone call, she and I were pulled out of the line and taken to a private booth.

"Tell Erick I said thanks," she said to the waiter and made herself comfortable.

It seemed as though she knew everyone, everywhere, and it made me wonder just how much power she truly had.

But I wasn't intimidated by her.

Nor was I inspired or in awe of her.

To be honest, I felt kind of sorry for her.

To date, in over two years, I'd never seen her with a man or even heard her mention one for that matter.

As stated, she didn't have kids so basically other than her business at the hotel, she was all alone.

No matter how much money, power, connections or whatever it was that she had, at the end of the day she was all alone.

None of the things that she had were even worth having if you had to be lonely behind them but I couldn't help but think that maybe she preferred things that way.

Yeah, I'm sure she did.

"Carmen, can I ask you a question?"

She didn't say anything, but her eye contact invited me to proceed.

"Why are you single?"

She looked at me as though I'd asked her for the combination to a safe.

I could tell that she didn't want to share the information, but she decided to anyway.

Maybe it was something that she wanted to get off of her chest or maybe she just wanted to hear my response to whatever it was that she was about to say.

"It's better this way. At least that's what I tell myself. But I wasn't always alone. I had someone that I really loved, once, a long time ago. But he left me for someone else and to be truthful, I don't think I've ever truly gotten over the betrayal. So, I don't get in relationships. I get what

I need from a man, sexually that is, and send him on his merry little way," Carmen explained.

It was hard for me to even picture Carmen in love.

She was just so nonchalant and bossy.

Basically, she was a bitch.

She was so difficult to deal with and I couldn't imagine how it must have been for the man who once loved her back.

To be honest, I could see why he would leave her.

Once the waiter returned and took our orders, I opened my mouth to ask her another question.

This one was about me.

The incident at my home the day after Christmas was one that could never, ever happen again.

"Remember when I started, I specifically told you that I couldn't sleep with any married men," I said just shy of a whisper.

"And I've kept my word. Or at least I have tried to," Carmen admitted it.

What the hell did she mean she *tried to*?

"Look, I told you I wouldn't knowingly set you up with a married man, and I haven't. But we both know that the clients lie about who they really are. There is just some information that is above my pay rate if you know what I mean. Seriously, we have one client that calls himself "Tuscan Sun" and we both know damn well that his mama didn't name him that. But as long as they have the funds, I do my part by making sure they get what they ordered and the people above me do theirs," Carmen faked a smile as the waiter placed our drinks on the table.

So, basically, every man that I'd ever laid down with could possibly, or in reality, actually be married.

So, there was no way to pin point the married ones or which client's wife was showing up at my house.

I guess that only leaves one option.

We were going to have to move.

But for me, moving was a big problem.

Moving out of my parents' house just wasn't in the plan.

I'd planned to raise a family there and grow old in the house, just as my parents had.

But I also had the safety of my daughter, sister and my nephew to think about and unless I got lucky and caught the person in the act, I didn't have any other options.

I guess was just one of those consequences for the decisions that I'd made.

And I was just going to have to deal with it.

***

An infant-sized dick was the worst!

My fake moans seemed to be just a little off but it was only because I couldn't exactly feel whatever it was that the client was supposed to be doing to me.

He was sweating, pumping and groaning away, and I was finding it difficult to stay focused on pretending.

I found myself moaning while he wasn't doing anything and I was hoping that he didn't catch on or sense how extremely bored I was.

It was Valentine's Day and I was just ready to get home to my Valentines.

Yes, against my better judgement, I was still seeing Silas.

Other than lying about his job and the one time that I'd spotted him at the hotel, he was perfect.

He done everything just right and I'd convinced myself to believe that he was hiding his profession for a reason.

Just like I was.

So, for now, I was simply going to go with the flow and I figured that we would cross that bridge whenever we got to it.

Being used every day only made me want to be wanted and loved, more, and for the time being, Silas was fulfilling that need.

Finally, the client collapsed on the bed behind me and I quickly scooted to the edge of the bed.

He reached a hand full of money in my direction as a tip and although I wasn't supposed to, I left the room before he did.

I would circle back around and clean up my room before I left.

"Envy?" Carmen said just as I was about to get into the shower.

I looked at her suspiciously.

She came closer to me although I was completely naked.

Her eyes quickly scanned every curve of my body and then she smiled at me.

"Do you have any plans tonight?" she asked.

"Um, yes I do actually. I have a date," I said to her.

I wrapped the towel around my body when I noticed that she couldn't keep her eyes off of my assets.

"Really? I didn't know that you were dating," she said.

Of course, she didn't know because I didn't tell her.

It was none of her business.

"Well, it's nothing to broadcast," I said to her and she simply nodded and turned her back to me.

What was that all about?

Thinking nothing more about it, I cleaned myself up, cleaned up *my room* and then I headed home in a hurry.

I arrived home to find that Silas was already there…and so were the police and the fire department.

In a panic, I ran to Tia who was sitting on the porch. Silas was holding Horizon.

As soon as she saw me, she stood to her feet.

"What happened?"

"I was sitting in the living room. I saw a car pull up and then a man got out of it. He had on a black jacket and sunglasses. I was about to head to the door but he pulled something from his back pocket. Before I could even blink, he lit the end of the cloth that was soaking inside of the bottle and he slung it through the living room window. My first instinct was to grab it and throw it back out the window, which I did, but not before it set the curtain and carpet on fire and burned my hand."

I looked down at Tia's hand.

It was burnt pretty badly.

This was crazy!

Things were really starting to get out of control!

I'd grown up in this house and had been living here for years, and never had anything like this ever happened.

Nothing like this had ever gone on…until I started sleeping with the men at the hotel.

We had guidelines.

What happened there was supposed to stay there, but it was obvious that someone hadn't followed the rules, and now my whole family was in danger.

Somebody was more than upset about something and at this point they were really trying to hurt me, and the ones that I loved.

If I didn't do something, soon, someone was going to end up hurt, or even dead, and it was going to be all because of me.

Silas forced me to tell the police the story that I'd told him the day after Christmas, when our cars had been vandalized.

Tia avoided eye contact.

She knew that the story was bogus and she knew that I was lying.

But she didn't say a word.

They prepared to take her away in the ambulance and as Silas continued talking to the police.

I stepped away to make a phone call.

If the hotel and the things that I did inside that hotel room was the cause of this, I had to eliminate the problem.

Contract or not, I couldn't risk the lives of my family any more than I already had.

"Yes Envy," Carmen said as though she didn't feel like being bothered.

"Carmen, look, for a while now I have been being harassed by one of the client's mates or wife or something. I'm not sure who it is but it has to be related to the hotel and one of the men that I've been with. I'm assuming one of my regulars. I don't know how, but they found out where I lived. They have been leaving notes stabbed to my front door and they even left their wedding rings in my mailbox. They've vandalized my car and I came home today to find that they had tried to burn my house down with my sister and my daughter still inside. Things are getting out of hand. My family is in danger," I said to her.

Carmen was quiet for a while.

"Envy, what are you telling me for? What do you want me to do about it? You already know the rules," she said.

Really?

I couldn't stand the way she thought about things!

Could she really be so cruel and cold-hearted that she didn't care about anyone other than those damn clients of hers?

"Well, do whatever you have to do, but I'm not sleeping with another one of those men. You can have every penny that I have but I can't do it anymore. This was the last straw," I said.

Without saying a word, Carmen hung up in my face.

I started to call her back but figured that I needed to join back in on the conversation between Silas and the police.

I took a deep breath and tried to get my mind together. This was all too much.

I hadn't told a soul so that meant that someone was breaking the rules and now things were getting out of hand.

Looking at Silas, I started heading towards him but a cop stepped in front of me.

He hung up his phone and then he looked at me.

"Envy Kirkpatrick, you are under the arrest for prostitution and grand larceny," he said as he started reciting my rights as he placed me in handcuffs.

What in the hell?

Carmen!

****
*

Chapter SEVEN

I rolled my eyes at Carmen as she led a new *maid* down the hall to a room.

Oh, I hated her with a passion!

Of course, she had been the one to have me arrested the day that my house almost burned down.

They put me in handcuffs and in the back of a police car like I was some kind of criminal or something.

I mean they took me to jail, booked me and everything!

All because of one phone call from Carmen.

After about an hour or so, Carmen showed up and wanted to chat.

Basically, she told me that either I was going to fulfill the duties of my contract, or I was going to have a very long night.

Still yet, I attempted to explain my situation to her, again, but she didn't seem to care.

She'd said that a deal was a deal and that I still owed her six more months and she expected just that.

After going back and forth for a while and seeing that everyone who was anyone was in her corner, I was released to her with no bail, paperwork or anything.

Once I was home that night, I lied and told Silas and Tia that I'd been taken in on an old warrant from my younger years but I assured them that everything was fine.

But things were not fine.

Things were a complete mess.

I was stuck being a whore whether I wanted to be or not and it didn't matter to Carmen whether my family was going to be hurt in the process.

I still didn't know who was behind the incidents but I was sure that they wouldn't stop.

My family wasn't safe and to top everything off I had to walk around lying about it all.

I was completely stressed out.

I was a fool to think that a whole year of opening up my legs to strangers wouldn't come with any problems.

I was angry for thinking that everything would remain a secret and that no one would ever find out what it was that I was doing on the thirteenth floor.

I guess that goes to show that some secrets are only as quiet as they were kept and someone was doing a whole lot of talking.

And from the looks of it, I'd been the topic of discussion.

My only choice now was to move my family somewhere safe and put my parents' house up for rent until things died down.

Shaking away my thoughts, I finished getting myself together for a client and when Carmen appeared, without a word, I rolled my eyes headed to my room.

Upon entering the room, immediately I wanted to burst into tears at the sight of the naked man, standing on the hotel bed, wearing only a cape and a cowboy hat but I knew that there was no time and no need to shed any tears.

It was clearer to me at that moment than it'd ever been before.

Without a shout of a doubt...I'd made the wrong choice.

***

I woke up to the satisfaction of Silas's tongue.

He could *lick the split*, like nobody's business.

Of course, some of the men at the hotel liked to go *down* on me, but I never actually paid attention to what they were doing down there.

Usually, my mind was somewhere else and I'd mastered the art of *faking it*, so they could never really tell the difference.

But with Silas, I was able to enjoy every bit of his tongue and what he was doing to me.

Things between us were still on pretty good terms and he'd been staying with us since the fire incident.

He'd said that he wasn't leaving until we moved.

I definitely felt safer with him around and I was sure that Tia felt the same way.

Trying to save herself and my daughter from a house fire, Tia pretty much burnt her right hand to the point of where it was useless.

She could still move it, but it was burned pretty badly.

She could no longer write with it so she was in the process of learning how to write with her left hand.

I felt so sorry for her.

I also felt guilty because I knew that it was all my fault.

But never, not even once, did she blame me.

She never really said anything about the incident at all or about the lie that I'd told the police about Keymar's other child's mother.

She was just happy that she'd seen it coming and that she had been able to save them and our parents' house as best as she could.

There hadn't been a whole lot of damage done to the house and the house insurance had covered it all and had already taken care of the damages.

All we had to do now was move.

"Envy, I love you," Silas said, interrupting my thoughts.

Though we showed it, neither of us had ever said the words.

Hearing him say them for the first time gave me butterflies.

I hadn't had a man say those words to me in such a long time and to be honest, it was like music to my ears.

It felt good.

It felt really good.

"I love you too," I said in a low voice and then tugged at his shoulders.

He understood what I wanted him to do and abruptly he stopped licking to position himself directly on top of me.

He stared into my eyes and I couldn't help but smile.

Though I was aware that there were some things that I didn't know about him, I was sure of the things that he showed me each and every day.

I was sure that he loved me.

I was sure that he cared about me.

I was sure that he wanted the best for me.

He showed it and I felt it in everything that he did and with everything that he said.

So, what if he had a few secrets, I had enough of my own.

As long as they weren't causing me any harm, I guess whatever it was really didn't matter.

Still smiling at him, strangely I started to think about my Daddy.

I was such a Daddy's girl.

Sure, I loved my Mama with all of my heart, but Daddy was my knight in shining armor.

I was his first child, so our bond was always pretty strong.

I would always stay up to wait for him when he would come home from being away in the service.

He would always assure me that he would go through hell and high waters to make sure that he made his way back home to me.

And he always kept his word.

Always.

I remembered being about thirteen and one day I came home from school early from feeling sick.

Mama of course was a teacher so she was working and since school was only around the corner from our house, with the clearance of Mama, I'd walked home.

Daddy was home from the military and I assumed that I was going to go home and be treated like his little princess and that he was going to take care of me until I felt better.

But Daddy was too busy taking care of someone else... his Army buddy; the man who we called Papa Pete.

Papa Pete was Daddy's best friend.

He and Daddy were as close as brothers and he loved us as though we were his own kids.

Obviously, Papa Pete's wife loved Daddy too.

Daddy and Pete's wife were going at it like wild animals and that was actually the first time I'd seen oral sex.

I couldn't believe that Daddy would do something to someone that was so close to him and to be honest, I was so disappointed in both of them.

He was such a respectable and loyal man.

He was my definition of what it meant to be a damn good man, but apparently, he was just like the rest.

They were both happily married and you would have thought that they adored their spouses.

But they were deceiving everyone that loved and cared about them and for that they both should have been ashamed.

I stood watching them for quite some time until finally they both noticed me.

I didn't require an explanation, though they both tried to cover up themselves and explain, but I didn't need to hear anything that they had to say.

I was the one that was going to do all of the talking.

I was clear about what they were supposed to do.

I was clear about what they had to do and made sure that they knew that they didn't have much of a choice.

Either they stopped doing what they were doing and never see each other again or I was going to expose them, ruin their reputations, and ruin their marriages.

Without hesitation, Daddy vowed that he would never speak to or see Papa Pete or his wife again.

He'd said that Pete deserved a much better friend then he could ever be.

I never saw Papa Pete or his wife again after that day.

Even when we got the news that Pete had died, Daddy didn't bother to go to the funeral.

I'd vowed to keep his little secret and I never said a word to Mama or anyone else.

It was just our little secret…and though he was dead and gone, it always would be.

I shook away the past as Silas kissed me.

He was good to me and I wasn't going to mess this up.

Hopefully his job was the only thing that he was lying to me about.

After all, we were in the same boat.

***

"Do you think that you'll be okay?" I said to Tia as she laid on the couch.

She was getting closer and closer to her due date and she was starting to feel a little pressure and hadn't been feeling her best the past few days.

"I'll be fine. Y'all have fun," she waved us off and turned her attention back to Horizon.

Silas and I smiled and we headed out the door to have some much-needed alone time.

I was being ordered at the hotel, every single work day, for the max of three times a day, for the past few weeks.

I was sure that Carmen had something to do with it.

I was sure that she was whispering the suggestion in some of the client's ear just to show me that she was in charge.

Sure, I was making plenty of money, but I was worn out.

And I knew that Carmen was behind it all because it seemed as though I was getting all new clients and they were all crazy as hell and requesting me to do something totally degrading and off the wall.

I mean they were requesting that I do the craziest of things such as licking their booty holes, *cuming* on my face and in my ears, all the way to wanting to insert objects into my *pussycat.*

And I won't even mention what one man tried to do to me with his toes.

I knew that Carmen was putting them up to it and I despised the sight of her.

She was just pure evil.

But we were at the beginning of April and I was almost at the finish line.

And I didn't care how powerful she was.

I promise, when my time was up, I was going to spank that ass and I was dead as serious about that.

She needed to be taken down a notch and I was the right one to do it.

Oh, I was going to whoop that ass.

Mark my words.

But tonight, was about Silas and I, so I was going to enjoy myself.

The hotel was out of sight and it was about to be out of mind.

We decided to do a movie first and then dinner.

I loved how Silas held my hand the whole time and how he often looked at me just to smile or to periodically kiss my forehead.

He made me feel like I was the luckiest, prettiest woman in the whole world and I was so appreciative of him.

After the movie, we arrived at dinner and he seemed a little tensed.

"Are you okay?" I asked him concerned.

"Yes, I've never been better," he said.

But I knew that he was lying.

I could tell by the way he avoided eye contact with me and how he often attempted to fix his attire, even though he knew nothing was wrong with it.

"Silas? Talk to me. You can tell me," I assured him, and he looked at me as if he was unsure if he could believe me or not.

Oh no, what's wrong?

I couldn't help but wonder if it had something to do with his "job" or if he was finally ready to confess that he was lying about it all in the first place.

Whatever it was, it had him as nervous as a stripper about to dance on a pole for the very first time.

"Silas?"

He looked at me and then he smiled.

"Well, if you insist," he said and got up from the table and got down on his knees.

I looked at him in shock.

"I know we haven't known each other all that long but I know that what I feel is real. I know that you are the best thing that has happened to me in a long time and I don't want to lose you. You can take your time. You can take a year or two to plan, as long as you say that one day in the near future, you will be my wife. Envy Kirkpatrick, will you marry me?" Silas finished his sentence and pulled out the ring.

I gasped at the sight of it.

It was freaking huge!

For the most part I couldn't believe that he was actually proposing to me.

I couldn't believe that in just a short time that he actually thought that I was the one.

He didn't really know me.

He didn't really know the real me.

He didn't know all of my secrets and all my flaws.

He didn't even know all of my truths so why on earth would he want to marry me?

I didn't know what to say so I started to cry.

Why was he doing this?

Why was he asking me something like this?

It seemed as though the entire restaurant was looking on, awaiting my answer.

Just then my phone started to ring.

It was Tia and out of fear that something might be wrong, I held up a finger in Silas's direction and answered the phone.

"Say yes Envy," Tia said.

"What? You knew?"

"Of course. Who do you think picked out the ring? I know it may seem sudden but he's good for you. And he loves you. Say yes Envy," she said in my ear.

Without even commenting to her, I hung up the phone and smiled at Silas.

I mean, we were going to have to have a long, heart to heart talk.

There were some things that we definitely needed to discuss and if we were going to be married, there were some things that we both needed to know.

I wasn't sure if I was going to tell him about the hotel since I only had a few more months to go but on the flip side of things I wanted to know what it was that he really did for a living.

What was I supposed to do?

I guess we could have a long engagement which would give us a little more time to get to know each other and for me to figure out if this was indeed the best decision for me.

But my mind was made up.

"Yes," I said.

Silas smiled and he gave me the biggest kiss that I'd ever received in my entire life.

The whole restaurant cheered and he placed the ring on my finger.

I stood to my feet and he gave me a long, lingering hug.

I started to scream and cry all at the same time.

I couldn't believe that this was happening!

The crowd's applause quieted down and everyone seemed to go back to enjoying their dinner.

Well...

"Wow, congratulations," I heard Carmen's voice behind me as she clapped her hands together slowly, sarcastically.

I looked at her in disgust.

Not today; she was not about to ruin this moment for me.

"Let me see the ring," she said and reached for my hand.

She looked at the ring as though she disapproved.

"You could have done a lot better," she said to Silas.

What?

Oh, no she didn't!

Who in the hell did she think that she was?

That's it!

She was all out of chances.

"Carmen, if I were you, I would leave," I said to her as I closed my eyes to keep from placing my hands around her neck.

How dare she say something like that to him?

"Envy, I'm just being honest. As much money as he has, he could have surely gotten you a better ring than that," she said.

What did she just say?

How does she know how much money he has?

Oh no, I was right...he was a client of the hotel!

I looked at Silas who hadn't said a word.

He was only staring at me.

"So, you know her?"

I waited on Silas to respond but Carmen responded instead.

"Of course, we know each other...he used to be my husband."

****

Chapter EIGHT

"Hey, do you feel like talking?" Tia asked.

I smiled at her and shook my head.

It seemed as though I just couldn't catch a break.

Out of all the men in the world, and in Charlotte, North Carolina, how on earth had I met the one man who had been dumb enough to marry a woman like Carmen?

I replayed the proposal night again in my head.

That night, Carmen went on to say that Silas had proposed to me in the same restaurant that he'd proposed to her in all of those years ago.

So much for feeling special!

She went on to say that he was rich and that his riches were related to his homeland, Africa.

She'd said that he'd never really told her if he was royalty or what, but she was sure that he was something to that extent.

She spoke of how he cheated on her and left her for another woman. He'd divorced her and remarried and she hated him.

The craziest part of it all was that the woman that he'd remarried...was Carmen's sister; who was deceased of course.

She'd never told me that one of her siblings had passed away, but now I see why she wouldn't have mentioned it.

There was so much anger in her voice and you could tell that she was somewhat happy about the fact that her sister and her niece had been killed.

When she'd told me that she'd been in love, once, I didn't think that she'd meant that she had been married.

But she had been…and to Silas.

My Silas.

The whole time she'd spoken that night, I was numb.

I couldn't talk, I could move.

I just stood there.

I just stared at her as if my look could cause her to have a heart attack or something.

The whole-time Silas hadn't said a word.

He only allowed Carmen to say what she wanted to say and then when she finally shut up and walked away, he didn't hesitate to grab my hand and lead me out of the restaurant.

But he still didn't say a word.

That night, we drove in silence.

I had no idea what to say.

I didn't even know where to begin.

All I could think was why me?

Why did all the bad stuff have to happen to me?

Why was it so hard for me to find happiness?

What was so wrong with me that I could never have it all?

Why couldn't I have the happily ever after like everyone else?

It just didn't seem fair; but then again, nothing in life was every truly fair.

There was always a winner…and a loser.

That's just the way that it was.

Since that night, I hadn't said much.

I hadn't said much to Silas *and* I hadn't gone to work at the hotel.

Surprisingly, Silas hadn't even asked me how I knew Carmen, but I was sure that it was coming.

At this point, hell, whether I told him the truth or a lie, it didn't really matter.

At least now he knew that I knew that he wasn't a doctor.

And now I understood why he always had more than enough money.

It was a lot to take in.

So, the question of the hour was…

Am I still going to get married?

The answer was that I didn't have a clue!

Sure, I loved him by now but he had been married to Carmen.

Out of all people he had been married to Carmen.

I still didn't know the whole story or even his side of the story.

I couldn't help but wonder why he'd cheated on Carmen and with her sister…what was he thinking?

I agree, Carmen was a bitch, but her sister?

That was just wrong!

One thing was for sure, and that was that his *character* was completely shot to shingles in my book.

I'd always known that there was more to him then what meets the eye, but never did I imagine that he had all of this in his past.

Carmen had been calling me non-stop to come in to the hotel but I said that I was sick.

She threatened me but I told her if she didn't believe me then she could fire me.

Even regular maids had sick days and whether she thought I was sick or not, I wasn't coming into the hotel.

If she didn't like it, she could terminate my contract and send me on my way.

But of course, she wasn't going to do that.

But I knew that I couldn't avoid her or Silas forever. I was going to have to face both of them eventually.

Later on, that evening, I decided that it was only right to talk to Silas first.

He hadn't been sleeping at the house with us and I would be lying if I said that I didn't miss his presence.

We all kind of missed him being around.

Horizon had asked for him on numerous occasions and I hated to see the look on her face when I told her that I wasn't sure when he would be coming back.

"Hey," he said at the sight of me.

I didn't respond.

I didn't know what to say or where to start so I allowed him to say something first.

"I hate that woman," he said.

Didn't we all?

But I didn't say anything aloud.

I waited for him to continue.

"I only married her so that I could stay in the states. It wasn't right. But at the time I was young and I was desperate for independence. I wanted to find my own way, despite being a part of family that was wealthy where I come from. I am the grandson of a king. But I wanted to stay here and start my life here. So, I met Carmen. At first I thought that maybe it was love, but it was impossible to love her. I tried but no matter what I did she gave me such a hard time. But time was running out so I married her although I knew that I shouldn't have. I tried to deal with her and my decision but she has her own issues that she needs to deal with and she was incapable of loving me. She's incapable of loving anyone other than herself. And then her sister started to come around. We didn't plan it. We didn't plan to fall in love. Despite what Carmen thinks, we never had sex until the divorce was final. Once the divorce was final and I was in the clear to remarry, I didn't hesitate and I married a woman that I loved more than life itself. We married and had a beautiful daughter together. It was the best decision that I ever made. I will never apologize for it. My family cut me off because they don't believe in divorce. Not to mention that they never wanted me to marry her or any other American woman in the first place. But I didn't care. It was my life and besides I'd always been smart with money so I'd made a few investments. I didn't need them or their money anymore and because of love, I haven't spoken to them in many, many years. Even after my wife and daughter died, there was nothing that I needed to say to them. I'm proud of the man that I've become on my own. Even before proposing to you, a while ago I'd visited Carmen at the hotel that she works for, just to apologize for hurting her. It's just the type of man that I am. I never thought that I would love again after the death of my last wife and daughter, and then I met you. Envy, despite my past, I love you. And I can make you happy, if you let me. I just want to make you happy," Silas concluded.

He'd said a mouth full and now I was even more confused.

It was a lot to take in and to be honest, to me, it wasn't all that bad.

I guess because I had a lot of secrets of my own that were far worse than anything he'd just said.

And at least now I knew why I'd seen him that day at the hotel.

I guess my biggest issue was going to be trying to stomach being with someone that Carmen used to be married to.

Now that was definitely going to be a hard pill to swallow.

Just the thought of it made me feel some kind of way.

But as I looked into his eyes, I could see that he loved me. I could see that he was still as sincere as he'd been the day that he'd asked me to be his wife.

Maybe I could try.

Maybe I could at least stick around for a little longer, just to see what happens.

I'd been by myself for the past three years and I wasn't in a hurry to go back to being alone.

I guess there was no harm in taking things one day at a time.

I shared my thoughts with Silas and told him that I couldn't make any promises but that we could see where things go.

But in the meantime, I was still going to wear my ring.

Yep, mostly just to piss Carmen off.

And besides, despite what Carmen said, I absolutely loved it!

***

"I'm sorry that I had to give you the bad news, but I had to let you know the type of man that you were dealing with," Carmen said.

The look on her face didn't say sorry at all; she seemed to be amused by it all.

I really couldn't stand her.

I was sick to death of her.

"You can do much better than him anyway," she said.

I purposely scratched my nose so that she could see that I was still wearing the engagement ring.

At the sight of it she rolled her eyes.

"Yes, thank you for sharing, but it's his past. I'm his future. Thanks though," I said to her and entered Room 313 to see what piece of a man was waiting for me.

I smiled but not at the sight of the man.

The look on Carmen's face when I'd said those words…

Priceless.

Another week or so had gone by and since I'd revealed that I was still seeing Silas, I hadn't been *ordered* or *reserved*.

Not even once.

I was sure that Carmen was trying to make sure that I didn't make any money, but I could have cared less.

I had more than enough money saved up and I was actually glad that I hadn't had to screw anyone other than Silas.

She was actually doing me a favor.

She walked around as if she hated the sight of me.

I was hoping that one day she'd finally do us both a favor and just rip up the contract and let me go.

My fingers were crossed.

After sitting around all day, it was finally time for me to go, so without a single word, to anybody, I made my exit.

It was such a beautiful day outside.

I was glad that the weather was starting to warm up because that meant that I was getting closer and closer to the date that I could leave the hotel!

Boy, I couldn't wait!

By now, I couldn't begin to count the number of men that I'd been with but I didn't even care.

When my time was over on the thirteenth floor, I was going to start over.

I was going to start brand new.

I arrived home and I'd hoped to find Silas there but he wasn't.

I still didn't know everything that he dabbled in because I hadn't asked.

To be honest, I felt that if I asked too many questions, he would start asking questions of his own.

He had yet to ask me how I knew Carmen and I had yet to get my lie together.

But I would be ready whenever he was.

I walked into the house to the sound of crying.

Both Horizon…and Tia were crying.

I ran to Tia's side.

She was bawling uncontrollably and Horizon seemed to only be crying because she was crying.

It's time!

"Aww, it hurts so bad! Get it out of me!" Tia screamed.

I almost smiled but she would have surely tried to knock my head off if I had.

I remembered those pains.

I found Horizon's shoes and helped Tia with hers.

I headed to her bedroom to grab her overnight bag and her purse and then I helped her out the door.

As Tia moaned and groaned, I made sure that the door was locked.

I turned back around to help her down the front steps but…

There stood a woman.

She looked as though she was drunk and as if she had been crying.

She stared in our direction as if we were her enemy.

By instinct, I grabbed Horizon and placed her behind me.

Tia continued to cry as we all just stood there, staring at each other.

I had no idea as to who the woman was but I was sure that I was about to find out.

The more I looked into her eyes, my gut told me that it was her; the one who had been coming by the house and the one responsible for all of the mysterious incidences, including trying to burn down the house.

I know that Tia said it was a man, but she could have surely put him up to it.

She was the woman whose ass I was supposed to whoop!

But now just wasn't the time.

I attempted to walk towards the car but she moved in front of us.

Tia cried out in pain again and I knew that we didn't have time to play around.

It was almost time to delivery this baby.

So, Lady, get the hell out of the way!

"So, you think you can just sleep with other people's husbands and get away with it?" she finally asked.

Damn it!

I knew that it was somebody's wife that was behind all of this.

I knew that one of the men at the hotel had made some kind of slip up and now their wife was pissed off and wanted answers.

But she wanted answers that I just couldn't give to her.

Especially not right now.

My sister was in labor.

"Look, I have to get her to the hospital. Come back in a few days and we can talk."

I tried to walk off again but she still wouldn't move out of our way.

Instead, she pulled out a gun.

My heart dropped as Tia and Horizon both began to cry even louder.

Was she serious?

Was this really happening?

Damn, okay, I get it, you're upset but to pull out a gun on me in front of my daughter...oh she was playing with fire!

I was getting more upset by the seconds and her best bet was to go ahead and shoot me because if she didn't...

"Look, we can talk about this some other time. Please just let me get my sister to the hospital, please."

The woman didn't say anything.

Instead she started to scream.

She was screaming at the top of her lungs like she was some crazy person.

It was almost unreal as though someone was playing a nasty joke on us, but I knew that she was serious.

I felt so bad for her.

Even though now wasn't the time to be feeling sympathetic, I still felt bad for her.

She must really love her husband…whoever he was.

Although in her mind I was just as guilty, I wanted to express to her that I never intentionally slept with her spouse, but I knew that she wasn't going to listen.

She started to mumble and then I heard the gun make a clicking noise which meant that she was preparing to shoot.

Was this really about to happen?

Was she really about to shoot me?

Was she going to do this in broad daylight, in front of my daughter, without hearing my side of the story?

I started to plea with her but I could tell that she didn't want to hear a word that I was saying.

Out of options, finally, I started to cry.

Not because I was scared, but because I hated that things had come to this.

That damn hotel was really about to cause me my life.

This was exactly why I didn't want to have sex with anyone that was married.

Knowing Carmen, all of the men she'd sent to my room were probably married and her messy ass probably had something to do with the wife finding out in the first place.

Carmen was capable of anything and I was sure that she was responsible for all of this.

If only the woman would let me explain.

But I knew that she wouldn't.

She held the gun tightly and when she put her finger on the trigger, I knew in my heart that she was going to shoot.

I knew that she had come to kill and I knew that she was going to do just that.

It was in her eyes.

It was all over her face.

Still holding on to Tia and with Horizon holding on to the back of my legs, I closed my eyes.

But at the sound of a car speeding into the driveway, I opened them.

Silas!

I had never been so happy to see someone in my entire life.

But the woman didn't look happy at all.

Instead she looked at him as he got out of the car and then with no more time to hesitate.

"He chose you. My husband chose you," she cried and with that the gun sounded and everything seemed to start going in slow motion.

Slowly I watched Silas start running towards the woman.

I wanted to move.

I wanted to hit the ground for cover, but I couldn't.

My feet were frozen.

My entire body was frozen in time.

So instead, I just waited for the bullet to hit me.

Slowly I waited.

And I waited.

And then....

I felt a huge weight on the left side of my body.

I struggled to keep my balance.

My eyes shifted to the woman who was now smiling as Silas bum rushed her to the ground.

Seconds later, the weight was gone and my arm felt as light as a feather.

And that's when it hit me.

She wasn't there for me.

The bullet was never for me.

Looking to my left, there on the ground, I saw Tia with a single shot to the head.

Dead.

****

*

Chapter NINE

I stared at Tia's body on the ground.

My mind and my body couldn't seem to get on the same page. Horizon actually made it to Tia before I did.

She was crying and begging Tia to get up, but Tia couldn't hear her.

So, this whole time everything had been going on because of Tia?

All of the incidents, the fire and everything were all because of Tia?

It was all starting to make since.

The woman was the wife of the married professor that Tia had slept with just to get enough money for us.

No, this was all my fault!

Tia was dead because of me!

Finally, my body came out of shock and I dropped to my knees beside Tia.

I held her in my arms and I spoke to her.

I shook her and tried to wake her but she wouldn't move.

She didn't respond.

She didn't do anything.

Tears started to fall from my eyes as the blood from Tia's head soaked the shirt that covered my breasts.

I held her close to my heart.

She just couldn't be dead.

My sister just couldn't be dead.

People filled the streets and some even ran into the yard and tried to help.

I could hear sirens in the distance so I was sure that someone had called for help.

I could hear Horizon crying and calling my name but I couldn't comfort her.

I couldn't do anything but hold Tia and cry.

I forced myself to look in the direction of Silas and once he made eye contact, he moved from restraining the woman and headed for Horizon.

No sooner than he'd headed in our direction, another gunshot ranged through the air.

The crowd screamed as two gentlemen rushed to the woman who was laying only a few feet away.

I didn't bother to look in her direction.

I already knew that she'd probably shot herself.

I hoped that she was dead.

She deserved to be dead.

I saw the blue lights in the distance and I was eager for them to get Tia to the hospital.

There just had to be a way to save her.

She just couldn't be dead...

"What are you going to name him?" Silas asked me.

I didn't bother to respond.

I just looked at my nephew through the glass window and cried.

He'd survived the shooting but his mother hadn't.

He was a beautiful, healthy baby boy and the saddest part of all was that he looked so much like Tia. It hurt me just to look at him.

Tia was pronounced dead on the scene.

There wasn't a thing that they could do for her.

The woman who had killed my sister and then shot herself hadn't died until later at the hospital.

I couldn't believe that she had taken something so precious away from me.

How could she kill her?

How could she shoot her right there like she was nothing?

It was confirmed that she was the wife of Tia's college professor.

Though he'd been notified, he had yet to show his face.

Why couldn't his married ass have stayed away from my sister?

Whether Tia called him that night or not, he should have been man enough to tell her no.

So, basically, it was just as much his fault for Tia's death as it was mine.

I cried and cried until there were no tears left in me.

I couldn't believe that my financial struggles had led to something like this.

Had I not needed the money, Tia would have never slept with him.

Had I not lost my job, Tia would have never tried to help me out.

Wait a minute...I should have never been fired in the first place!

Carmen was just as much to blame as the rest of us.

She'd fired me for nothing.

All because I'd initially refused her offer to sell my body.

Yes, that bitch was to blame for this too!

As far as I was concerned, everyone was a fault!

But blaming folks wouldn't bring my sister back.

No matter what I said or who I blamed, she was gone and nothing was going to bring her back.

"Envy."

I turned around at the sound of her voice.

My sister Josephine looked so different that I hardly even recognized her.

I hadn't seen her in person since Keymar's funeral, over three years ago, and it was sad that if she hadn't said my name, I probably wouldn't have known who she was.

She was darker and she was about a hundred pounds heavier.

Her hair was even different.

She didn't look like herself at all.

Immediately she hugged me and we cried together.

She asked me what seemed like a thousand questions but I only answered one.

The wife of her child's father shot and killed her.

The end.

After all, that's all that pretty much mattered.

Though Josephine hadn't noticed him at all, Silas decided to take Horizon to the cafeteria to give us some alone time.

"Why was she sleeping with a married man?" Josephine as though she was disgusted.

It was as if she was looking down on Tia and it was almost as if she understood why the wife had killed her in the first place.

No, I'm not saying that sleeping with the married man was right, it wasn't.

But it was only one time and it was only to help me.

Tia hadn't deserved to die because of it.

I was so angry at myself.

I was the one that should have been dead, not her.

I scowled to myself for being frozen in shock.

I should have jumped in front of that bullet.

Heaven knows I would have taken that bullet for her.

Josephine continued to talk but I tuned her out and focused on my other sister heading towards us.

Sonni looked as beautiful as she always had.

She and I actually favored the most.

But though we looked alike, we didn't have a thing in common; never had.

She was the child that was always different.

She would rather read instead of playing outside or while everyone would be playing together, she would be somewhere in a corner, sitting, and playing all alone.

Sonni had never been to close with anyone of us. We used to think something was wrong with us because on most days, she wouldn't even talk to us.

I mean not one single word.

She just liked being alone and her own little space and no matter how much we tried, that's just the way that she was.

It was as though she was ashamed of us or as if she just didn't like us or most people for that matter.

Actually, I couldn't believe that she'd even gotten married or had kids.

I would have never guessed that she would have let someone that close to her.

As soon as Sonni graduated high school, she took off for a while.

At one point she was in Texas, then New York and then somewhere in California.

She dabbled in a few things and became very good with advertisement.

After she'd gotten skills and had become adored in the industry, she headed back to North Carolina, settled about four hours away from Charlotte, and soon she went into business with a gentleman, who eventually became her husband.

Their business was pretty successful I suppose.

I didn't know much about it and of course Sonni didn't share much of anything with any of us.

It seemed like the only person she'd ever really talked to or even liked was Mama.

And well, obviously, her husband and kids I guess.

Once she was close enough, surprisingly she reached out to hug us.

She wasn't crying but I could tell that she was hurting.

"What happened to her?"

I gave her the same answer that I'd given Josephine, only this time I went more into detail.

I told them both about the incidents at the house and that Tia had only messed around with the husband on one occasion.

I left out the fact that she'd done it for money.

I was already feeling guilty enough, so I didn't need anyone else blaming me for what happened to her.

"I was just thinking about you guys. All of you. I'd just talked about how we needed to do better as sisters and that our kids needed to know each other and spend more time together."

I was surprised to hear those words come out of Sonni's mouth.

But I was glad to hear them because with Tia gone, I was going to need both of them more than ever.

Tia had become my best friend.

She had been my only friend.

What was I going to do without her?

"I'll pay for everything," Sonni said but I shook my head.

"No, I got it. I want to pay for it all," I said, still in disbelief that I was actually discussing my sister's death.

"Can you afford to do that? Are you still at the hotel?" Sonni asked.

I thought about lying.

I surely knew that I couldn't tell her the truth, so I said whatever I felt like saying.

"No, my fiancée and I will pay for it," I said to them.

At my words, they both looked at my hand.

My ring was ten times bigger than both of theirs and both of their mouths dropped open at the sight of the diamond on my finger.

"Congratulations! When? Who? Why didn't you tell us?" Josephine frowned.

"As she said, we have to do better as sisters," I said and we all group hugged.

"Excuse me," a voice said behind me.

I turned around to face the voice, which belonged to a man whom I didn't recognized.

But though I'd never seen him, just from the look on his face, I already knew who he was.

He was the husband.

"This is all your fault," I said to him, although I knew that it wasn't.

At first he didn't say anything.

He took a seat and placed his hands on his head.

"If you had a wife at home, why even have sex with her? Why?"

"My wife and I were separated at the time. After she'd lost our third child, we just couldn't seem to get back on the right track. So, we took some time apart. To be honest, I thought that we were headed towards divorce, but only a few days after having sex with Tia, she came by and wanted to reconcile. I had no idea that Tia was going to be pregnant and when she called me and told me, I tried to fix it," he said.

"What? Tia was pregnant?" Josephine asked and I pointed towards the glass.

Both Josephine and Sonni headed to take a look at the baby.

They cooed and as a result of their reaction, the man stood and headed to see the baby as well.

It wasn't until he saw him that he broke down.

His cries filled the halls of the hospital and they were filled with so much pain and agony that they pierced my soul.

I'd never seen a grown man cry; at least not like that.

His cries were so painful, so excruciating that his crying made the rest of us start crying too.

"I tried to fix it. I told her that I'd gone back to my wife and I offered to take care of it, but she wanted to keep it. She said that she would raise the baby on her own and for a while I didn't hear or inquire anything else about it. But a few months in, I'd seen her on campus and I couldn't help but say something to her. I told her that I wanted to be apart but she told me no. I started making sure she'd ate and I started going by her classes but she didn't want anything to do with me. One day, she was about to leave and I saw her and tried to talk about it with her again. The thing was that my wife had come to bring me lunch and she saw me touch Tia's stomach. Once Tia was gone, she approached me and asked me about Tia and I didn't have a choice but to tell her the truth. I told her that it was while we were separated but what hurt her the most was that Tia was pregnant. She couldn't seem to carry a baby full term but now another woman was carrying my child and it seemed to be too much for her to handle. She left me… again. She didn't talk to me and I thought for sure that all she wanted was a divorce. She kept asking if I wanted Tia to keep the baby, and when I'd told her yes and that I'd had a change of heart, she kept saying that I was choosing Tia over her. I didn't know how bad it really bothered her. Whenever I tried to talk to her about it, she never wanted to discuss it. I had no idea that she was capable of something like this. I had no idea that she was going to kill her and then kill herself. I just can't believe that something like this happened," he managed to spit out all while still crying.

Everyone was at a loss of words.

The only thing any of us seemed to be able to do was cry.

I guess I could see why the wife went crazy.

I remembered how I felt finding out that Keymar had another child so I could only imagine how she felt.

She couldn't have a baby and now her husband was having a baby with someone else…that might've made me a little crazy too.

But she should have simply tried to talk about it or gone to therapy or something.

Killing my sister was the last thing that should have been on her mind.

Hell, why didn't she just kill her husband instead?

To me, that would have made more sense.

But then again, Tia was the one who had what she wanted...a baby.

After the crying stopped, we all just stood silently and looked at the baby.

Though he was the father, the baby was going home with me.

I was sure that he had rights to him, but that little boy was the only thing that I had left of Tia and I needed him at home with me.

I was hoping that he wouldn't put me through any kind of custody battle because I would do what I had to do to make sure that he would lose.

Silas and Horizon appeared and I officially introduced him to my sisters.

They seemed to approve of him and then they loved on their niece whom they hadn't seen since she was a little baby.

It was sad that only death seemed to bring us together but hopefully nothing else would keep us apart.

It was time that things changed.

Whether they needed me or not, I was going to need them more than ever.

I was going to need my sisters.

***

Tia's funeral was one of the hardest days of my life.

I felt as though I'd lost a child.

It felt as though I was burying my daughter.

Once they closed her casket, I knew at that very moment that things were never going to be the same.

I could feel a change happening within me and I was sad to say that it wasn't a good thing.

I was angry.

I was hurt.

It seemed as though everybody that I cared about always ended up dead and it just wasn't fair.

I'd told her not to do anything stupid.

I'd told her that I didn't need her help.

But she hadn't listened and now she was dead.

Nolan, the husband and Tia's son's father, sat a few spaces from me, holding the baby.

Though he was his father, he agreed to let me keep him but he promised to do his part as a father.

I had no idea what I was going to do with another baby but I felt as though it was my duty to raise him for my sister.

I'd allowed Nolan to make him a junior and I could already tell that he was going to be an amazing dad.

After all, he and his wife had been trying to have a child their entire marriage, so of course he'd always wanted a kid.

He'd said that he couldn't believe that he'd tried to talk Tia into an abortion and you could tell that the baby already had his heart.

His wife's funeral had been the day before.

I'd wanted to go and spit on her body, but Silas wouldn't let me out of his sight.

I could tell that Nolan was overwhelmed but he was trying to keep himself together.

The guilt that he felt showed all over his face, but he wasn't the only one responsible.

We'd all played a part.

Silas was right by my side like he had been the entire time.

He had been so helpful through the whole process and I was so thankful for him.

To be honest, if he hadn't been there to help me, I would have surely gone crazy by now.

Silas was just a blessing.

He was willing to help me with the baby.

He was already helping me with Horizon.

He was heaven sent and I couldn't wait to be his wife.

It was nothing like a tragedy to help you make a few decisions, and no matter who he had been married to, sooner or later, he was going to be married to me.

We stood as they prepared to take her casket out of the church.

I smiled at my sister's husbands and my oldest nephews.

I couldn't believe how much they'd grown and how different everyone looked.

My sisters were on my other side and we'd all made a vow that we were going to keep in touch and at least make time to hang with each other once or twice a month.

It was sad that it took a death to get us back on the right track but I was just glad that we were going to try.

The casket and the fellas exited the church and my eyes noticed a familiar face.

Carmen.

What the hell was she doing here?

She surely hadn't been invited.

I'd only spoken to her once and that conversation hadn't gone that well.

I'd ended up cursing her out and making a few threats that I surely planned to keep.

Carmen was more concerned about when I could come back to the hotel, more than she was concerned about me or the death of my sister.

She was the true definition of what it meant to be *money greedy.*

She'd agreed to give me a month off to get everything situated, but of course she was adding the month to the end of my contract.

I was so sick of her and the hotel that it wasn't even funny.

With the new baby and with Tia gone, I had no idea how I was even going to be able to work there.

I had more important things to worry about and popping my pussy for a *fee* wasn't one of them.

But all Carmen cared about was when she could tell her clients that I would be back.

She'd said that they were begging for an exact return date so that they could pay top dollar to *reserve my curves.*

There just had to be a way out.

There was always a way out.

Passing by her and heading out of the church, I decided that I just might have to take my chances with the law.

But then again, the law was already on her side.

What was I going to do?

****

Chapter TEN

Getting up in the middle of the night with a crying baby was no joke!

I'd forgotten about the sleepless nights and all of the work that was involved with tending to a new born baby.

Silas tried to help when he could, but most of the time he slept on the couch just to get a decent night's rest.

Nolan and I had come to an agreement.

On the days that I had to work at the hotel he would keep him and on the days that I was off, I would have him.

Since I still had a few days before I had to go back, the baby was with me, and had been the whole month, in hopes that I would have better luck getting him on some kind of schedule but so far, this baby did whatever it was that he wanted to do.

But tired and all, I did what I had to do with minimum complaints, because I was the reason that he didn't have a mother.

I missed Tia so much that it made my stomach hurt but I was doing a lot better than expected.

I guess since the baby kept me busy, I didn't have a lot of time to mourn and grieve the way that I wanted to.

But I guess that was a good thing.

I was going to have to accept the fact that she was gone and she wasn't coming back.

But it just wasn't easy.

Finally getting the baby to sleep, I fell asleep soon after and I dreamt of the future.

There, I was married to Silas of course and we had a house full of kids. Horizon was all grown up and so was the baby.

We were celebrating and all of my family was there.

Everyone was happy.

Everyone was smiling.

Life was good.

If only my dream would come true.

***

"How are you doing?" Josephine asked.

I loved the fact that we were talking regularly.

I'd forgotten how much fun she could be.

Sonni was doing better with calling as well and from the looks of it, we were all in this together, and it really felt good.

"I'm fine. My first day back at work is tomorrow, so I'm getting the baby ready to go with Nolan."

"Work? I thought you said that you weren't working at the hotel anymore?"

Did I say that?

I tried to replay the conversation at the hospital that day.

Maybe I did say it.

"Did I? Oh, no, I didn't mean to say that I didn't work there. I still do. I guess I was just saying that Silas had enough money for us to cover the funeral," I tried to explain.

In reality I'd been the one to pay for everything.

I'd bought every single thing for Tia's funeral and everything had been nothing but the best.

But I was fine with letting everyone else think that Silas had done it all.

Though he'd offered to help and had more than enough money to contribute, I'd refused.

It was my responsibility.

"Oh, well, maybe I can get the baby for you guys sometime next week," Josephine said.

Josephine and her husband had four kids.

Her youngest was the same age as Horizon but if she wanted to join in on a few of those sleepless nights, who was I to stop her?

We continued to make small talk and then a knock came at the door.

Hanging up with her, I answered it, knowing exactly who it was.

Nolan.

"Hey, is he ready?" he asked.

Nolan was maybe in his late thirties or early forties.

He looked damn good for his age though and I could tell that in his younger years he was probably a hot commodity.

He appeared to be a pretty decent guy.

We hardly ever got the chance to really hold a conversation, so I figured that today was just as good as any.

"Yes, he's ready…well, almost," I laughed.

Nolan closed the door behind him and followed me down the hallway to my bedroom.

Silas was out doing whatever it was that he did and Horizon hadn't moved from in front of the TV.

I grabbed the baby from the crib and laid him on the bed.

He had been napping, so I finished dressing him with care.

"So, how have you been holding up?" I asked him.

I could see that he didn't really want to talk about the situation, but he answered anyway.

"I'm taking things one day at a time. But for the most part, I'm fine," he said with a smile.

I nodded and pointed to the babies socks so that he could reach them to me.

Instead of handing them to me, he proceeded to put them on the baby's feet and as he reached across me, I got a whiff of the scent of his skin.

Why did that just turn me on?

He smelled so good that my mouth started to water.

No, this wasn't right and I scolded myself mentally, but for some reason as his arm continued to brush up against mine, I found myself getting more and more aroused.

Envy, stop it! Get it together.

I shook my head and got my hormones in check.

Nolan finally finished and stood to the side to allow me to put on the baby's shoes.

Once everything was done, I handed him his son and placed the diaper bag on my arm.

We headed up the hall and although I didn't turn around, I could tell that he was walking extremely too close.

It was as if he wanted to place his dick on my ass but he didn't want to cross the line.

I couldn't deny that both attraction and maybe even a little inappropriate tension were in the air, but we both knew that that was a line that we just couldn't cross.

He told me that he would bring the baby back in four days and he went on his way.

Biting my bottom lip as he pulled out of the driveway, I shook away the impure thoughts that were trying to creep into my mind.

It didn't take long for me to get focused.

I had to get Horizon dressed, dropped off at daycare, and then I had to get to the hotel.

And boy was that the last place that I wanted to be.

"Envy, so how is everything at home?" Carmen asked.

I failed to realize why she insisted on trying to talk to me about anything other than business.

She knew that I didn't like her and she knew that I didn't want to be there, let alone talking to her.

But even though I couldn't choose not to be at the hotel, I wasn't going to pretend like everything was okay.

It wasn't.

"Do I have someone already in *my* room?" I asked her bluntly.

She looked at me as though she wanted to say something sarcastic but I guess she decided against it.

"Yes, one of your regulars. And you've been *reserved* for the last four hours of your shift. I guess you've been missed," Carmen said.

I nodded and headed to get myself together.

"Oh, and by the way, the *no* married men thing is out the window. Due to high demand and the fact that every married client that we have seems to be drooling over you, I can no longer accommodate your request. I hope that you understand. It's nothing personal. It's just business."

Carmen walked away like the bitch that she was.

I guessed she thought that she was hurting me but the truth was...she wasn't.

At this point, I didn't care whether the men were married or not.

The way that I felt in the inside was cold and heartless.

I didn't care about much of anything or anybody, except my family and of course Silas.

Though I knew that it was wrong and that sleeping with a married man had cost my sister her life, I now looked at things differently.

Husbands that cheat on their wives were a disgrace and in some way, they deserved to pay.

And not just financially.

What's the one thing that all men loved?

Sex.

What's the one thing that could cause even the smartest man to make the dumbest mistakes?

Pussy.

I was going to freak the hell out of these married fools and then send them back home to their boring wives.

I was going to make them feel so good yet so bad in the end because the one thing that they were going to want more than anything in the world, one day they wouldn't be able to have…

Me.

Yes, I was going to use them, take their money, and in just a few months I was going to be gone and they were still going to have to deal with and face the fact that somewhere in their lives, homes, marriages, or bedrooms, something was still lacking.

It was going to be sad when the wives realized that they had their husband's physically; but mentally, sexually and emotionally…their husband's chose me.

He chose the big girl.

Their husbands' heart and dick would yearn for the woman that most of them probably looked down on, made fun of, or looked at as though they were better than them because they weighed less.

But in the end, weight wouldn't matter.

And in the end, that was going to be their problems, not mine.

They were still going to be pathetic and unsatisfied, while I was going to be happy and damn near rich.

It all sounded pretty good to me.

I headed down the hall to my room with a whole new frame of mind.

It was time to show these men who was in charge.

Just because they had the big bucks, I had the big butt, and they weren't the ones running the show.

I was.

And it was time that they recognized that.

There was a new bitch in town and from here on out, things were going to be a lot different behind the door of 313.

Yep...it was time for these trifling so called men to pay...and what they couldn't pay with money, later they would pay with misery.

Let the games begin...again!

***

"I love you," the client said.

I wanted to laugh aloud but I knew better than to do that.

He didn't love me; he only loved how I made him feel.

Slowly, I rocked back and forth with his *manhood* inside of me.

I allowed the muscles of my vagina to squeeze the life out of his penis, as his moans filled the air.

He was one of my new married clients.

He had been coming to see me twice a week for the past month and I was making sure that every single time I put it on him.

After all he was flying all the way in from Florida.

Oh yeah, he was good and *whipped!*

From what he'd told me, he had been married for about five years.

His excuse was that his wife only wanted him for his money and that having sex with her was like a punishment.

He said that usually she laid there like a dead corpse and that half of the time he didn't even *get his rocks off*, for lack of a better phrase.

Oh, but when he came to see me, I made sure that he was satisfied…at least twice was my goal.

I was going to enjoy knowing the sadness that he would feel on the day that he came looking for me, and I was nowhere to be found.

He was surely going to be disappointed because my end date was right around the corner.

And I had been *sexing* him really good too and had him giving me all his damn money.

I couldn't even begin to count the amount of money that I'd received in tips from him and a few other married men that I was giving the business to too.

I had them giving me more money as a tip than the cuts that I received from Carmen for the services.

By the time, it was all said and done, I was going to be a *set* bitch, and I probably wouldn't be going back to work for a very long time.

I'd dropped my classes at the college.

I figured that I could always go back and finish.

I just didn't have the time.

My main focus was finishing out my days at the hotel and then I could figure my life out from there.

"Damn, this feels so good," the client said.

He was right…it did.

I tried not to enjoy it most of the time, but sometimes I just couldn't help myself.

Especially with him.

The hook in his penis got me every time.

My juices flowed and my body temperature started to rise.

He gripped my waist, firmly, and I closed my eyes.

I forcefully began to thrust my hips in a circular motion, but he stayed with me.

I found myself moaning and I knew that an explosive orgasm was right around the corner.

He pulled me close to his chest and we continued to rock to an unheard beat and before we were both quite ready, we exploded together in unison.

Rolling off of him, I waited for him to catch his breath and pull himself together so that I could change the sheets on the bed.

Glancing at the clock, I only had about an hour before my next client was scheduled to arrive and I wanted to spend majority of that time, soaking in a hot bath.

The client dressed and then approached me and poked out his lips for a kiss.

Ugh...I am not your wife!

What on earth made him think that I actually wanted to kiss him?

But knowing that a huge tip would follow, I gave him one hell of a kiss, and just as I expected, he gave me one hell of a big tip.

He left the room and I started to clean.

Well, at least Carmen had been right about one thing.

Married men do tip the best…

Later that evening, I arrived home to find that Nolan was already there waiting for me.

I was so exhausted but I still had other obligations.

Though I was off for the next three days, I still had to tend to my motherly duties to Horizon and the baby, and I had to make sure that I showed Silas some attention as well.

Silas was starting to pressure me for a wedding date.

The truth was that I didn't want to start planning until I was done with the hotel.

That way I could start brand new and I wouldn't have anything to hide.

I'd told him that in less than three months I was going to be leaving the hotel for good.

He'd said that he liked that idea and that he could take care of all of us.

But the truth was that I didn't need him to take care of me.

I had so much money stashed in my closet that I was sure that with or without anyone, I was going to be fine for a while.

I needed to find a way to get it in an account.

I had no idea how I would be able to explain that much money.

But anything could happen.

Had that fire actually spread through the house, I would have lost all of the money that I had stashed at that time.

Nolan smiled at me and started to get the baby and his things out of the car.

As far as I knew, he was still teaching at the college.

His family members helped him with the baby on the days that he had him.

Everything was working out just fine.

"How was work?" he asked me.

His question caught me by surprise.

I guess he figured that we might as well become well acquainted since we were going to be in each other's lives for a very long time.

Just as I opened my mouth to answer him, my phone ranged.

"Hey baby," I smiled.

"Hey, baby. Are you off? Do you want me to pick up Horizon?" Silas asked.

To date, I still didn't know what he did all day but he did finally admit that he wasn't a doctor.

Though I'd known it for a while, to hear him say it made me feel like he was really starting to put his trust in me.

He asked for my forgiveness for lying.

He'd said that he had always wanted to be a doctor but all of his different investments had kept him busy for the last few years.

He mentioned that he was caught up in stocks and other things but that was about it.

He talked a while longer and stated that he would pick up Horizon, grab a movie and dinner and that he would be there shortly.

Nolan followed me into the house carrying the baby and his things.

I smiled as I looked at junior.

He was starting to look less like Tia and more like Nolan every day.

He was sleeping with a smile on his face and I grabbed my cell phone to take a picture.

Nolan noticed and snapped a few pictures of his own.

As he pretended to be focusing on the baby, I caught him checking out my body.

Oh man, here we go.

"So, I'll be here to get him on Monday," he said as I walked him back to the door.

I smiled at him and he smiled back.

Something told me to shut the door, but I guess I didn't move fast enough.

Before I had a chance to do anything, Nolan kissed me…and I kissed him back.

****
*****

Chapter ELEVEN

It was Horizon's birthday and unlike the year before when I was broke and hadn't even celebrated it, this year I'd gone all out.

I had clowns, bouncers, princesses, cotton candy machines, ponies…everything.

Anything that you could name was there and Horizon was having the time of her life.

I was also happy because my sisters, their husbands and all of their kids were in attendance.

It felt so good for us all to be together again.

Life just didn't get any better than this.

I headed into the house to get some more sodas.

"Envy."

Nolan was standing by the counter in the kitchen.

Of course, he'd been invited because of the baby, but the baby wasn't the only one that he was there to see.

Nolan and I had been screwing each other every chance that we could.

In a way, I felt terrible being that he was Tia's son's father but in another way, strangely, it kind of made me feel closer to her.

I know that it sounded weird but for the life of me I couldn't control myself when I was near him.

I also felt bad for cheating on Silas.

That man was so damn good to me.

"Nolan, Silas is here. Everyone is here," I said backing away from him as he inched closer.

He didn't say anything.

He only smiled.

Only inches away, he took his right hand and rubbed the outside of my thigh.

Instinctively, I slightly moved my legs apart and he placed his hand under my dress and rubbed my awaiting pussy.

As he caressed my clitoris, my juices soaked his fingers and I stared deep into his eyes.

"Envy?"

At the sound of my name, we both jumped and Nolan took the sodas out of my hand.

He smiled at my sister and headed back outside.

Josephine stared at me as she walked closer.

I smiled as if I was innocent.

"What was that?" Josephine asked.

"What was what?"

"That?"

"I don't know what you're talking about," I turned my back to her and started to pick up things of the counter.

"You two have something going on, don't you?" she asked me.

I looked at her as if she'd insulted me.

"No, why would you say something like that?"

Josephine just looked at me.

"Um huh, whatever you say. We all got secrets girl," she said.

Boy, ain't that the truth!

"Secrets? I don't have any secrets."

"Humph, well, I guess you would be the first," she said and helped me gather the rest of the things from the counter.

Now I was curious.

"Josephine, you have secrets? Yeah right," I giggled.

She grinned at me slyly.

Josephine was such a plain Jane.

Her secrets were probably something stupid.

"Okay, you tell me one of your secrets, and I'll tell you one of mine," I bribed her as we walked towards the back door.

She looked at me as if she was trying to figure out if she could trust me.

She shrugged and then she said:

"You're not the only one sleeping with someone that's been with one of your sisters. I've been sleeping with Sonni's husband for years."

What!

***

"Are you and my ex-husband still seeing each other? Do you ever think about the things that he used to do to me while he's doing them to you?" Carmen asked.

This bitch here just doesn't stop!

I knew that she was just trying to get under my skin but I wasn't going to let her.

"Nope. From my understanding, having sex with you was like having sex with somebody's mother. Trust me our sex is on a whole different level. If I were you, I would get over it already. Just like he'd chosen her over you back then…your husband, well your ex-husband, now chooses me," I said to her and walked away.

That should teach her ass to mind her own damn business!

Now, I had to get myself together.

I was seeing a new client today.

Carmen said that he wanted kinky and that he wanted the works.

I hardly ever asked if they were married anymore, because it no longer mattered.

I was hoping that he was sexy and spontaneous because I was in the mood to really get down and dirty.

I'd been keeping a *healthy* distance from Nolan and Silas was sick with a bad summer cold for the whole three days that I had been off, so I was definitely in the mood for something that was going to make me feel good.

I didn't bother to put on a sexy maid outfit, since kinky was what he'd ordered.

Instead, I put on a black laced thong, a matching bra, a rip it off of me short pink dress and some black Gucci, suede pumps.

With handcuffs, a whip and a jar of peanut butter, I headed to my room.

Hopefully he would enjoy my peanut butter trick.

They all enjoyed the peanut butter trick.

"So, what do you want me to do?" I asked him.

I could tell that he was nervous.

I tried to rub his shoulders in hopes of relaxing him but he was still so tensed.

He was fairly attractive so I was hoping that he loosened up soon so that I could see what he was working with.

"What do you want me to do?" I asked him again.

He looked at me.

He was hesitant for a moment but finally he spoke.

"Well, for starters, bitch, I would like for you to stop sleeping with my husband," *he* said.

Wait a minute...

What?

To Be Continued...

PART TWO THE FINALE NOW AVAILABLE ON AMAZON!

JOIN MY BOOK GROUP

My Book Group:

https://www.facebook.com/groups/authorbmhardin/

Author B.M. Hardin's contact info:

TEXT BMBOOKS to 22828 for more release updates

Facebook: http://www.facbook.com/authorbm

Twitter: @BMHardin1

Instagram: @bm_hardin

Email:bmhardinbooks@gmail.com